THE CORONA VERSES

ALSO BY TIM O'LEARY

Nonfiction

Warriors, Workers, Whiners & Weasels

Fiction

Dick Cheney Shot Me in the Face, And Other Tales of Men in Pain

Men Behaving Badly

THE CORONA VERSES

Stories by

TIM O'LEARY

RARE BIRD
LOS ANGELES, CALIF.

THIS IS A GENUINE RARE BIRD BOOK

Rare Bird Books
6044 North Figueroa Street
Los Angeles, California 90042
rarebirdbooks.com

FIRST PAPERBACK EDITION 2025

For more information, address:
Rare Bird Books Subsidiary Rights Department
6044 North Figueroa Street
Los Angeles, California 90042

Set in Minion
Printed in the United States

10 9 8 7 6 5 4 3 2 1

Library of Congress Cataloging-in-Publication Data available upon request

FOREWORD

I was in New York City when the first chatter of Corona began.

"Nothing to worry about," the President assured us. I was unconvinced. I've had a lifelong tussle with hypochondria, battling the dread and odd delight of imagining every pain is life-threatening. Combined with my love of apocalyptic tales, the idea of a world-wide pandemic overwhelmed me. I returned home to California, where I selfishly hoarded Costco-branded toilet paper, a flat of Kirkland tuna, pasta, a fifty-pound bag of rice, Lysol wipes, AAA batteries, and took refuge with my wife Michelle and our dog to tend garden at our solar-powered rural retreat.

We installed theater seating and a massive Samsung television in our tiny den and subscribed to every available streaming service, quickly binge-watching the entire run of *Game of Thrones*, *The Wire*, and a French police drama I still can't pronounce. We adapted the British tradition of "sundowners," our official five p.m. cocktail hour, mixing martinis and gin and tonics like 1960's suburban alcoholics. Anticipating a potential food shortage, we stretched normal meals across several days, with incredible leftover innovation. But despite the threat of food scarcity, we treated ourselves to elaborate desserts, with the justification that you can't enjoy brownies and homemade ice cream after you're dead. We gained weight. A lot of weight.

The most essential people in our lives now piloted trucks, delivering everything imaginable to shield us from the danger of human contact. We worshipped at the Amazon alter and were constantly amazed at what could be shipped right to the house: homemade pasta sauce from someone's garage in Brooklyn, salmon caught a day earlier in Alaska, pomegranate flavored gin from Italy.

Two months into the plague, fearing our own mental deterioration from isolation, we constructed a "bubble of friends" whom we communed with on a weekly basis. Qualifications for the bubble included:

1. Reasonable paranoia.
2. A serious embrace of mask culture.
3. The propensity to wash your hands with a surgeon's zeal on an hourly basis.
4. A well-stocked bar and willingness to share.

Preference was given to childless couples, or at least those whose kids were grown and not at home, to avoid contact-by-extension with an entire coughing third-grade class. Gatherings were held in our backyard, surrounded by twenty treed acres, with couples assigned to their own tables, all spaced twelve feet apart. Donning masks, we greeted each other with quick elbow bumps before retreating into safe spaces.

As tests became available, we asked guests to shove Q-tips up their noses before entering the premises. Nobody was allowed inside the house, except for one remote bathroom, equipped with a MERV 7 Hepa filtration system, the space meticulously sanitized at the end of the evening. We preferred to meet on breezy days, theorizing that diseased droplets would blow high into the canyon. The group learned the art of communicating via yelling, like deaf old men shouting salutations across the driveway. In one particularly shameful episode, I screamed, "Are you trying to kill me?" at a friend when she admitted violating the bubble to go swimming outdoors with non-bubble friends.

We regarded every surface with suspicion, wondering how long the killer virus would live on marble, cardboard, or the plastic wrapper that encased the hand sanitizer we whipped out every time we entered a room. Can you catch it from a doorknob or car hood? Was it transmissible via broccoli spears?

We debated mask efficacy, attempting to translate Chinese and Korean N95 designations. Initially, cloth masks covered with funny sayings and designer logos provided a touch of fashion to our otherwise bland "running suit" wardrobes, until we discovered they didn't work and might actually be harboring disease. Just as the bright red MAGA hat was a symbol of a Trumper, the mask became a political and social statement for those who considered themselves medically enlightened and responsible, and the mask/no mask controversy quickly erupted into a new social battle that sometimes ended with bloodshed.

When the vaccine first became available, we drew a little closer to share harrowed adventures locating the difficult-to-find elixir; shots as hard to procure as Taylor Swift tickets. I received an urgent text from a friend informing me that Pfizer had just become available at a senior center in Lompoc, California. Another friend drove almost three hundred miles from Northern California to a CVS Drugstore in Ventura to get jabbed. My wife ventured into the bowels of a suburban Walmart forty miles away to be poked with Moderna by a woman with questionable medical credentials. We proudly displayed our vaccination cards, which we incorrectly assumed made us bulletproof against the plague.

Now it all seems like a dream; times so weird it occurred to me we might actually be living in a video game. Cue the reality-show President, white supremacists marching on American streets, the threat of Jewish space lasers and baby-eating celebrities, while tech billionaires flew around the universe like Bond villains.

The silliness of many of our actions is not lost on me. But we've quickly forgotten the uncertainty at the onset of Corona. Would it morph into something so deadly we would all exist in a Charlton Heston movie? Should we douse our Amazon deliveries in Lysol? What are the medical implications of Clorox enemas or snorting Tide?

Corona is a shapeshifter. Now, an affliction (at least for the time being) more akin to a bad flu than a pandemic, but also a failed social experiment. It turns out humans don't do well in isolation, especially when fed a steady stream of digital pablum, misinformation, and media incentivized to make us angry. The damage extends far beyond health implications, as it divided families and inflicted a tremendous social, political, and economic toll that makes it easy to forget Corona has so far killed almost seven million people.

I'd been working on a novel but could no longer concentrate on that particular fiction with the drama unfolding around me so much more compelling. I abandoned the book, and, for the next two years, concentrated on the following stories, each loosely inspired by real-life events. They are snapshots. Some sad, some humorous and uplifting, and a few ridiculous. Many echo the loneliness that Corona exacerbated. They emanate from the fictional town of Santa Pulmo, where the characters occasionally intersect. And like Covid, these tales never really end, but I hope they serve as some kind of entertaining record of the first two years of the disease.

Terry Hughes, Moshe Schulman, and the Portland Writer's Group gave great advice on many of these stories, and there is nobody I would have rather quarantined with than my wonderful wife Michelle.

I hope you enjoy!

VERSES

Verse I

FOUR POUNDS OF ASHES

NELSON WAS IN THE kitchen when he heard the chirp. Not a bird: something mechanical and urgent. "I hope it's not that damn smoke alarm again," he muttered to his dog Sparky and tried to calculate the last time he had changed the battery. It was a dangerous endeavor, perching sky-high on a ladder, arms windmilling for balance, while sliding a square nine-volt into a flimsy plastic house. It couldn't have been more than three months ago, he figured, but time moved differently during Corona. One endless day. Imagine surviving the plague only to break your neck repairing something designed to save you. They might not find his body for months. If he was lucky, Al, the UPS driver—the only breathing soul he encountered these days—might peer through the window when the boxes began to stack-up on the porch.

No, not the smoke alarm, he realized when he reached the den. The racket was emanating from his iPad. Nelson had an aversion to technology, but he had ordered the thing from Amazon to read. The little screen, he discovered during the pandemic, was not only a literary device, but also a window to happier times. Every afternoon at four p.m., fist wrapped around a tumbler of Glenfiddich, he would fall back into the La-Z-Boy, prop the iPad on a pillow on his lap, and enjoy a couple of hours of video comfort food. He would often doze off, rising at six or seven to refill his glass and pop one of the prepared meals he'd ordered online into the microwave.

As he turned on the device, he didn't know what to make of the message flashing: JESSIE B. WOULD LIKE TO FACETIME. He turned to Sparky. “What in the hell is FaceTime, and who is Jessie B? Some Nigerian calling to ask for my Social Security number?” Sparky watched him for a moment, and then moved to a rug to lie down. “Maybe I’ll give him the number from your dog tag.”

As he fumbled with the device, the screen filled with a woman’s image. “Nelson, is that you?” she asked.

The face was familiar, but Nelson couldn’t place her. “Who is this?”

“Nelson, its Jessie Burdett. I hope you remember me. I owned Wordstock, the bookstore.”

Ah, Jessie Burdett. A bubbly woman, suspiciously kind, usually clad in mom jeans and T-shirts with feminist slogans: WOMEN WHO READ LEAD. He’d spent hours in Wordstock, often soliciting Jessie’s literary suggestions, though they sometimes led to good-natured debates. She adored science fiction, which he deemed useless. A retired history professor, Nelson had limited use for all fiction. Real life provided all the drama he needed, especially now. She also had some musical talent. He’d seen her sing at the local dinner theater.

Nelson clearly recalled her.

He looked for a button on the iPad, wondering how to respond. *Does it work like a walkie-talkie?* “Jessie. Hello. Can you hear me?”

“Yes, Nelson. I hear you, but the picture is shaky. I’m looking at your ceiling. Hold it up so I can see you.”

See me?

Nelson hadn’t been seen in a long time, especially by a woman. Patting down his hair and attempting a smile, he raised the iPad at arm’s length, grimacing when he saw his image at the corner of the screen.

“There you are. Hello. Did I catch you at an okay time?” She was sitting at a kitchen table, somewhere sunny, light flooding the yellow wall behind her.

Nelson smiled. “I have a busy schedule here. Walk the dog. Eventually, I need to pop one of those TV dinners into the microwave, which takes a couple minutes. I guess I could spare, I don't know, two or three hours."

Jessie laughed. "Would you like to get more comfortable? It looks like you're standing and holding up your pad, which can't be easy. Take a seat."

He sat down at the desk, and fumbled to prop the iPad against a book, adjusting the screen until they could both see each other.

"Sorry, first time," he apologized. "If we get disconnected, you'll need to call me back, since I have no idea how to do it. Reminds me of *Star Trek*. Though, as you know, I'm not a science fiction fan."

"Isn't it wonderful?" Jessie said. "I'm surprised you haven't used this to talk to your family."

Nelson clenched his jaw. "No family to speak of anymore."

"No?" Jessie looked confused.

"It was just my wife and daughter. You met them. Cassie would come in the store with me sometimes, and my daughter Liz loved your shop. She was a bookaholic, just like her dad. But...well, I lost them both to the virus."

"Oh my God," Jessie said. "They were lovely. I'm so sorry."

"Thanks." Nelson's voice dropped. Why talk about it to someone he barely knew? "Happened early. Cassie had gone to San Francisco to visit Liz right before it started. Liz had just graduated from medical school and was doing her internship at Saint Francis Memorial when it hit. Don't believe them when they say it only kills old people," he snorted. "Liz got an extra big dose, working in the hospital. Both were quarantined but never made it out. I wasn't even allowed to visit. Never saw them again."

"Oh, Nelson, that's terrible."

"You know what they do?" he continued, welling up. "They ship the ashes back to you, UPS. Imagine that. Al shows up one morning and hands me three boxes. One filled with printer ribbons, another dog treats, and the third held my wife and daughter in fancy tin cans. Eight pounds of ashes."

"Oh no, Nelson."

"Learn something every day. Sometimes things you don't want to know. The average woman's ashes weigh about four pounds. Did you know that?"

"No, I didn't."

"Why would you?" He shook his head. "But I was glad to have them back. Wouldn't want them spending eternity on a shelf in San Francisco. They both loved it here. There's a big field behind the house where we liked to ride. Melton Creek runs across the south side of my property. I spread their ashes there. I think they would like that."

"I'm sure they would."

"Even had a funeral for them, or at least the best I could put together under the circumstances. I called our neighbors, and all the friends I could get ahold of, and they met us there for a Covid-safe ceremony. Al the UPS man even came. The girls liked Al. Said he reminded them of Santa. Big, fat, happy, and always bringing presents." Nelson chuckled. "Everyone stayed back at the edge of the field, and we all said goodbye. A few folks from the church even came and sang a bit."

"That sounds lovely, Nelson. Melton Creek is beautiful. I have many wonderful memories of that area. In fact, when I die, that's exactly where I'd like to spend eternity."

"Oh Christ, I apologize." He waved a hand. "Hell of a thing to bring up when we haven't talked for so long. It's just…I haven't spoken to anyone in a while, unless you count the dog." He moved the screen so Sparky appeared in the background. "We have long conversations. Argue politics. Sparky is a socialist. He thinks we should share all the food evenly. Especially when I serve steak."

Jessie laughed. "No apologies needed. The last time I remember seeing you was a month or two before the virus hit. That seems like a lifetime ago."

“Sure does,” Nelson said. “Amazing, isn’t it? Everything is going along fine, and then someone somewhere decides that a monkey or bat would make for a tasty dinner, and the world comes to a standstill.” He discreetly wiped an eye and sat up in his chair. “Enough sad talk. Tell me about yourself, Jessie.”

“Doing okay,” she said, “all things considered. A month after I closed Wordstock, I moved to Santa Barbara to live with my daughter Julie. She lost her husband. He was a dentist but volunteered to help during the worst of it. He went from saving people to being one of the patients, just like your daughter.”

“Oh, Jessie,” Nelson shook his head. “I’m sorry to hear that. My condolences.”

“We’re getting along fine,” she said. “She has two little ones and works from home, so she needed the help. I tutor the kids and keep them occupied.”

Nelson contemplated what it would be like to have a child in the house; the joy he had taken for granted. He avoided going into Liz’s old room. Sometimes, on his morning horseback ride, he would see the Owens kids running through their field. He’d stop to watch—careful not to get too close.

“May I ask? How did you reach me on the FaceTime thing?”

“I had your cell number in my contacts. Remember, I used to call to tell you when a book you ordered came in? All you need to FaceTime is a cell number.”

“You’re calling to tell me that the Robert Caro biography I ordered finally arrived?” Nelson asked.

“I forgot, you did order that,” Jessie laughed. “You should be thanking me. How much can one person read about LBJ? So, what *are* you reading these days?”

“That’s why you contacted me? To learn what I was reading?”

“Sort of.” Jessie hesitated for a moment. “I miss the store. I miss talking to my customers. I decided to go through my address book and get ahold of a few people. This seems like a good time for people to talk, even if it isn't in person. I started alphabetically. Quite a few of the A's through C's have disappeared. It frightens me, wondering whether they just gave up their number, or perhaps the virus got them. However, you came up quickly, Mr. Nelson Daniels. I really used to enjoy our discussions, even though I think we should broaden your literary horizons. The way the world is right now, I just crave smart people."

For the next hour they talked books, politics, music, movies—intent on occupying a more normal place for a change. At one point, Jessie suggested they take a bathroom break and grab a cocktail.

"During the quarantine, it's always five o'clock," she joked, which led to a discussion of Corona alcoholism and the pending baby boom, as she sipped from a glass of wine, and Nelson enjoyed a scotch. An hour later, she moved closer to her screen and frowned. "Oops, time to recharge the battery, and I better get to work on dinner."

Nelson felt a surge of panic. "Really?" he said, noticing his battery was low, too. "Jessie, I really enjoyed this. Do you suppose we could do it again?"

"I was thinking the same thing," she said. "How about dinner tomorrow night?"

"Dinner?"

"Tomorrow at six p.m. I will call you. We will both be sitting at our dining room tables with our meals and some wine. Find a good spot to set your screen, like the seat across from you where I would sit, but make sure I can see you, and we'll dine together."

That night, Nelson opted not to drink himself to sleep. A belly full of scotch tended to give him night sweats and uncomfortable encounters with ghosts, which translated to feed bags under his eyes the next morning. He wanted to look good for his date.

Was it a date? He wondered.

The next day after he finished his chores, he showered, shaved, and made a misguided attempt at trimming his hair. Instead of his normal sweatpants and a tattered Santa Pulmo State University sweatshirt, he donned chinos, a white button-down, and his blue blazer. He seldom drank wine but found a bottle of cabernet in the cabinet. Someone had written "Happy Anniversary" in gold pen on the bottle, and flashing to their anniversary party two years earlier, he shoved it back on the shelf as if it were contagious. He had a clear memory of this very room filled with friends, many bearing gifts of wine, and now he felt guilty. It didn't seem right to drink their anniversary vino with another woman, even though Jessie wouldn't really be drinking it. He stood and paced. Maybe he should call this whole thing off. It felt like cheating.

Sparky eyed him from his bed. "So, what do you think about me dating? Is it nuts?" he asked, as if the dog might answer. "Christ, I guess I can't spend the rest of my life just talking to you," he said, leaning down to rub Sparky's ears. He returned to the cabinet and found a bottle of pinot noir that he knew wasn't a gift.

For the first time since his wife had left, he set the table, spreading the blue tablecloth formerly reserved for holidays and a matching cloth napkin. Instead of eating his microwave meal out of the plastic container, he positioned the food across a China plate.

At 5:55 p.m., he was sitting across the table from his iPad, staring at the dark screen, wincing whenever he saw his image reflected. He jumped up when it flashed JESSIE B. WOULD LIKE TO FACETIME.

"Good evening," he shouted as he pushed the button, not knowing the range of the microphone. Jessie was wearing a green blouse, her hair pulled back into a ponytail, looking fresh. She had moved into a dining room, with a real meal sitting in front of her: roast pork, rice, salad, and wine chilling in a bucket to her right.

"Hey, you cleanup nice," she said, smiling. "Very handsome."

Nelson wondered if she could see him blush onscreen. "Don't know about that, but you look beautiful. Thanks for joining me."

"What's on your menu?" she asked, insisting he tilt the screen toward his plate.

“I don’t cook,” Nelson said defensively, “but I unpack well.” He laughed. “These premade meals show up in a big box once a week. They aren’t bad.”

“Oh, Nelson. I bet they’re full of chemicals. One of the joys of Corona is having time to cook. I’m going to give you cooking lessons. I’ll turn you into a real chef.”

Nelson had no desire to be in the kitchen, but the idea of more time with Jessie thrilled him. They spent the next two hours engaged in a surprisingly normal dinner that extended to dessert. Jessie returned to the camera with a freshly baked cookie and an espresso. The best Nelson could do was an ancient Baby Ruth bar purchased for a long-past Halloween placed on a chipped coffee saucer and served with a cup of Keurig decaf. Jessie laughed at the candy and pledged to send him a box of baked treats.

They decided his cooking lessons would commence on the following Thursday. Nelson put in a grocery order to Whole Foods, waving at the gloved and masked deliveryman through the window, clad in a T-shirt that said, PLEASE STAY BACK SIX FEET, like a sign you would see on a fire truck.

Nelson mounted the screen on a shelf that afforded a complete view of the kitchen, and Jessie talked him through chicken piccata, wild rice, and a salad with homemade dressing. After the preparation, they dined together, ending the meal with brownies Jessie had shipped a day earlier.

Soon, the cooking classes became a regular Tuesday and Thursday event. They started an online two-person book club: Jessie guiding Nelson through Philip K. Dick, Robert Heinlein, and William Gibson, while he insisted she read Doris Kerns Goodwin, Jon Meacham, and Walter Isaacson. Next came yoga lessons, with Jessie demonstrating downward dog. “The key to aging well is to stay flexible,” she counseled. Nelson just tried to hide his admiration for the sight of her in stretch pants.

Six weeks later, after a cooking lesson that produced penne with homemade seafood sauce, served with a bottle of Barolo Nelson ordered online (he'd shipped a duplicate order to Jessie), Nelson decided it might be the right time to ask.

"Jessie, you ever think about coming back?"

"To Santa Pulmo?" she said. "I'd love to, someday. I grew up there and consider it my home, but I don't think there will be a demand for a bookstore anytime soon. Right now, living with my daughter works financially. Between the two of us, we can afford one household."

Nelson nodded, deciding this was the appropriate time to bring up what he had been considering for the last week. "Well, I have a four-bedroom house on three acres of land. Seems a shame to occupy all this space by myself."

Jessie's mouth opened in surprise. "Nelson, are you serious? You're asking me to move in?"

He didn't know how to answer. Was he taking things too quickly? What were the relationship rules during Corona?

"Well, yes. I mean, I have all this room. And I think my cooking and yoga skills would advance a lot faster if my teacher was onsite," he joked.

"But my daughter and grandkids—"

"Bring them," he interrupted. "The more the merrier. Plenty of space. The kids can play with Sparky and ride horses. I have a big den we can make into a fine office for Julie. Fast internet, too. I can help tutor the kids. I guarantee they will get A's in history, and they'll also be experts on Lyndon Baines Johnson, which probably won't add to their popularity, but will help get them into a better college. When things get back to normal, you'll be in good shape to reopen Wordstock. I bet people will love going back into bookstores."

Jessie smiled but looked shocked. "Nelson, I have to say your invitation is sweet, but a total surprise. Are you sure you could handle a house full of women?

Nelson had been thinking of nothing else the last few days. "I would love to have a full house, if you're part of it. The last few weeks...well, it's the first time I've felt alive since this all began."

"I've loved it too," she said. "But it's a huge decision. For all of us. I need to really think about it and talk to the family. I want you to give it a lot more thought, too. It would be a big change for you. It's one thing to talk online, but you'd be surrounded twenty-four hours a day."

"I'd love that," Nelson said. "But no pressure at all. It's just an option to consider."

"I appreciate the invitation, and Julie and I will discuss it," Jessie assured him.

When they hung up ten minutes later, Nelson turned to Sparky. "What do you think, old dog? Did I screw that up, or is she interested?"

That night, Nelson slept poorly, watching the clock while wondering how early he could FaceTime. He rose at five a.m., fed the horses, drank too much coffee, paced the house, and finally decided ten a.m. was reasonable. Jessie answered right away. "Good morning," she said, smiling. She was putting on a coat and appeared to be leaving the house.

"Good morning. How are you?" he asked.

"Slept in this morning," she said. "I was a little tired. Maybe too much wine, and now I'm running late. Can we talk later tonight?"

"Sure," he said, not relishing a whole day of not knowing. After dinner, he tried to FaceTime, but she didn't pick up. "Just seeing how you're doing," he texted. He kept the phone and iPad by his bed, waking up several times during the night to see if she had responded.

The next morning, feeling panicked, he tried again and left a voice mail and a text. *Jessie, if I came on too strong the other night, I apologize. I don't want to scare you off, and we can take all this as fast or slow as you'd like.*

Another day passed with no word from her. Was she ghosting him? He'd read about the phenomenon in *The New Yorker*. He couldn't imagine that she would just decide to cut off contact. It seemed too cruel for Jessie, but then she probably wasn't used to some old man she barely knew coming on so strong, and these days that might be how it's done.

He waited three more days, now wondering if he should be worried or offended. He called directory assistance to see if Julie had a landline, but there wasn't a listing. He considered his options. He was tempted to grab Sparky, jump in his truck, and drive to Santa Barbara. It would be tricky. They might have quarantine restrictions entering the city, but he figured he could find a way through. That evening when he tried calling again, he received a message that the phone was no longer in service. Terrible news, and it left him with no idea what to do.

He had scared her off, and he couldn't blame her. He'd acted like a lovesick teenager, pressuring her to move in with him when they hadn't even been in the same room together for over a year, much less shared a kiss. "I must have been out of my damn mind," he said to Sparky, as he crawled back into the La-Z-Boy with a full glass, quickly reverting to bad habits. "Guess we'll just be two old bachelors," he said to the dog, the familiar sadness rolling over him.

Three weeks later, he was sitting on his porch when the UPS truck pulled up. Al crawled out the back and set a box at the base of the stairs. He waved at Nelson. "Morning," he said brightly. "Have a great day."

Nelson grabbed the Lysol he kept on the porch to spray down packages but stopped when he saw the Santa Barbara postmark. Ripping it open, he recognized the tin container. There was a card with an obituary notice stuffed inside and a note from Julie.

Nelson, so sorry we never had the opportunity to meet, but Mom spoke so highly of you. She thought she had beaten the virus, but it overtook her, and we lost her very quickly. She had a weak heart, and Covid was the final straw. You should know that you brought a lot of joy to her last few weeks. While she was sick, she spoke of how much she wanted to get better so she could return to you and Santa Pulmo. I know this is probably a surprising request, but she asked that I forward her ashes to you. She said you had discussed it, and it would be the greatest gift in the world if you and Al could spread them along Melton Creek. Someday, when the world has healed, the girls and I would love to visit her there. Hopefully, this isn't too much of an imposition. Thank you so much and stay well. I pray someday we can meet and celebrate her life together with a picnic on the banks of the creek. Julie

Nelson carried the tin into the house and set it in the center of the coffee table. That evening he slumped in his chair and stared at the four-pound box while he consumed most of a bottle of scotch. Sometimes he wondered if the last year was even real. He felt like he was living some other version of his life, an alternative reality from one of Jessie's damn science fiction books.

Two days later, he and Sparky were sitting on the porch when the big brown truck rumbled down the driveway. That morning he'd cleaned up, once again donning his blue blazer. Al yelled a greeting, and then stopped when he saw the tin box sitting on the step next to a wrapped bouquet of flowers.

"Morning, Al," Nelson whispered. "I was hoping you could spare a little time today. We've been invited to a funeral."

Verse II
BLAME DREAMY McPOTSY

RILEY SWERVED HER MIDNIGHT onyx Range Rover around slow-moving traffic, leaning on the horn while screaming, "What the fuck? Is Miss Daisy in the backseat?" She hated being late for her eleven a.m. pilates class, which meant being relegated to the rear row of reformers, ancient clunky metal machines that creaked and stank of bleached vinyl. Riley feared contracting an infection from touching the foul things.

When she arrived at Penny Pilates, the door was bolted, a sign taped to the glass. DUE TO THE GOVERNOR'S STAY-AT-HOME ORDER, WE WILL BE CLOSED UNTIL FURTHER NOTICE. PLEASE VISIT OUR YOUTUBE CHANNEL, PERFECT BOD BY PENNY.

Closed? Riley was on week three of the Fan-Asstic series, spending every morning sideways to the mirror, pinging her rump as if thumping a cantaloupe. Any interruption was unacceptable.

She wondered if this was a legal issue. Perhaps Penny hadn't been paying her taxes and the IRS had closed her down. Being blessed with a pole dancer's flexibility did not make you a good businesswoman.

Pulling a U-turn, she snagged a handicapped spot in front of Lazy Owl Coffee & Scones. This situation called for a large skinny macchiato and some serious Googling to find a new studio. However, the shop was closed, a sign citing the same government mandate, while offering home scone delivery from the owner's son, mentioning he would be wearing a mask.

Why would I want someone in a mask coming to my house? At least not to deliver scones, she considered lasciviously. She glanced up and down the street, which was suspiciously empty. She saw a woman locking the door at Wordstock, the bookstore next to the Lazy Owl. She recognized her as the owner. Maybe Jenny or Jessie. Riley was not much of a reader, but she enjoyed the magazine rack at Wordstock, preferring print when lying next to the pool. Suntan lotion could be hell on a Kindle.

"Hey, hey," Riley yelled, approaching the woman. Jenny or Jessie stopped, careful to keep the car between the two of them. "Why is everything shut down?"

The woman frowned. "The stay-at-home order. All businesses need to close." When Riley appeared baffled, she added, "Because of Corona."

"The beer?" Riley asked. *Had there been a Mexican-beer-based food poisoning?* "You're closed because of beer?"

"My business just shut down, but I'm glad you can find humor in the situation."

Riley watched the woman drive off in her Prius. She turned when she heard a rumble and crunching gravel—a UPS truck pulling up across the street. An addicted online shopper, she had a close relationship with Al, the driver.

Hustling across the street, she yelled, "Hey, hey, Al!"

He stepped back as she approached him and held his hands in a defensive position.

"Hi, Riley. Six feet back, please. It's a company rule for your safety."

"Al, why are all the businesses closed?"

"Haven't you read the Governor's order? All non-essential businesses are shut down due to Corona."

"What in the hell is Corona?"

"You don't know about it? Seriously?"

Riley was more into Instagram and YouTube than the news, but this was sounding familiar. She'd read a few posts warning of some new virus, but it had not seemed like a big deal. Just something happening in China that the president said would not be a problem here. She sped home and spent the next two hours online, horrified to discover what was happening in the world. How could everything be shutting down, just when she was looking so damn fine? A few minutes later, her phone buzzed with a text from Dennis, her "friend" from New York. She'd been planning a shopping trip to the Big Apple, and he had tickets to *Mean Girls* and a late reservation at Dirty French.

"SORRY BEAUTIFUL. TRIP CANCELLED THANKS TO THE DAMN CHINESE FLU. HEADING TO QUARANTINE IN CONNECTICUT WITH THE BALL AND CHAIN."

This really was serious!

She called her housekeeper, Debra, instructing her to go to Whole Foods and quadruple their normal weekly order. "No, more than that. Ten times what we normally buy. Fill the freezer and pantry. And toilet paper," she shouted. "Buy all of it!" She'd read about all the selfish people hoarding, and she didn't want to be caught empty-handed.

Since she was wearing her best Prana, she decided to try to work out in the home gym but couldn't concentrate. Without someone yelling instructions, she tended to sit motionless on the Peloton and watch TV, locked in place by the Real Housewives' botoxed faces.

An hour later, perched in front of the refrigerator and contemplating the ideal smoothie, Randall shocked her back into reality by saying hello. She jumped and recoiled when he planted a kiss on her cheek.

"What are you doing here?" she asked. "I thought you were in Seattle all week." Riley did a quick house inspection in her head, wondering if she had left anything incriminating lying around. She hoped the bed didn't reek of the god-awful Dior Sauvage Danny the lawn boy insisted on wearing. "It doesn't make you smell like

Johnny Depp," she complained, not convinced that Johnny Depp even smelled good. He had that dirty boy look.

"They closed the office. I decided I'd better get home before this thing gets any worse. Looks like we're going to be quarantining for a while."

Christ, Riley thought. *I hadn't thought about that.* It was one thing not being able to go out, but spending weeks cooped up with Randall sounded awful.

"I'm going to unpack and change," he said, kissing her again. "Then let's have a drink and talk about how we're going to handle all this togetherness. It might be good for us. Let's make it fun."

Riley fumed. Randall's idea of fun was playing board games and watching old movies. She hated Scrabble. If she wanted to spell, she would have gone to college. And she couldn't stand an evening watching DeNiro, Hoffman, and all those ancient fucks he loved so much. Her stomach churned at the scent of Randall's old-man pine shampoo, probably for dandruff. She detested his oversized Tommy Bahama sweater and baggy chinos—grandpa clothes.

Riley had underestimated the challenges of being with a man twenty-five-years her senior. She'd figured that with all his money anything would be tolerable, especially since he was on the road for business most of the time. She could even recall a time when she'd been attracted to Randall. Her friend Claudia commented that he was the same age as George Clooney. However, Randall was no Clooney. *She* was the only interest they shared. Music suddenly blared from the living room. *JamesfuckingTaylor.* Randall populated the Sonos playlists with decrepit songs from his youth, forcing her to wear earplugs to avoid the yacht rock racket.

She retreated to the patio with her laptop to learn more about this Corona thing, pleased to discover it was primarily affecting oldsters. She figured it was reasonable to trim the herd a bit. Riley considered herself an environmentalist, and a reduction in population could be a positive thing—*as long as they were older than sixty*. Randall was a couple years shy of the danger zone but did have occasional bouts of hay fever, which upped his risk profile. As the spouse of a high-risk individual, it seemed wise to emotionally prepare herself for the worst.

Randall handed her a glass of chardonnay. "Join me in the kitchen to cook dinner?"

"Cook?" She frowned at his outfit. He'd changed into some kind of velvet tracksuit Tony Soprano would find stylish.

"During quarantine, I don't want anyone in the house," Randall said, "I told Debra not to show up until further notice. We're going to have to brush up on our cooking skills."

"I don't cook. The best thing I make is reservations," Riley said. "You knew that when we got married."

"It's lucky that I do. C'mon, I'll give you a lesson. If I die of Corona, you'll need to know how to make dinner," he joked.

I should be so lucky.

"We're also going to have to do our own cleaning until this thing is over."

Clean? She didn't get married to become a goddamn maid. This Corona thing might end up cramping her style.

~

Two weeks later, isolation depression challenging her sanity, Riley was panicked to discover she was almost out of pot. Since being quarantined, she'd doubled down on her consumption. *What if the shops were closed?* She went online to Speedy Weedy, relieved to learn they were not only operating as an essential business but also running a promotion on her favorite vaping cartridges: Raspberry Kushpa and Dreamy McPotsy. An hour later, she was standing inside her front gate, a text notifying her the deliveryman was arriving.

This must be him, Riley surmised as she inspected the rusty Toyota Tercel. It was missing the front bumper, but this was not a vehicle worthy of protection with the doors wavy with dents and a sheet of black plastic covering the passenger window.

A man jumped out, wearing a welder's mask and what appeared to be a kid's Halloween costume version of an astronaut's uniform. Instead of boots, his feet were encased in bright blue Crocs.

"Riley?" The question muffled under the plastic faceplate.

"Hey, hey."

He placed a small sack on the ground and pointed a bottle of Lysol kitchen cleaner at it. "Disinfect?" he asked.

"No!" Riley yelled. "Don't get that on my cartridges. Take off the mask. I can't understand you."

He expelled a big "thanks," as he pulled off the helmet, and slid her bag through the gate. "This thing is cool looking but damn hot. Don't worry. I'm immune to the virus. They make me wear this so the customers feel better."

"You look freaky. Why are you immune?"

"Already had it. Got it early on. Did you read about the outbreak at Moonlight Cove? The old folks home?"

Riley did remember coming across that when she was researching Corona. "Yeah. Didn't a lot of people die?"

"Sure did," he said. "I was working there as an orderly, and the whole place blew up with Corona. Twelve out of the fifty that lived there passed away."

"Ugh. Poor old people. They're fragile. That's sad. But you came through it okay?"

"Wasn't bad. Sore throat and a cough for about a week. Then I was fine. I got this job, which I like a lot better. People need pot during the pandemic, so I feel like I'm doing something important. Plus, the roads are empty, so it's easy to get around."

Riley inspected him more closely. Early twenties and looked to be in good shape—though it was hard to tell through the baggy outfit. Scruffy, but kind of handsome in a "dirty fuck" sort of way. She wasn't accustomed to going this long without an outlet for her oversized libido. Randall was always willing, but he snored like a motherfucker, talked with his mouth full, and strutted around in those old-man jeans he thought made him look sexy.

"Hey, Randall," she'd kid him—and not in a nice way, "David Hasselhoff called. He wants his pants back." Why did old men always talk about their health, like she was fascinated by what foods gave him acid reflex or gas?

The truth was, she loved younger guys. The younger, the better. Danny the lawn boy was barely eighteen, and while his lack of experience could be annoying, he made up for it with enthusiasm and energy. Plus, he was obviously in love with her, which felt good.

"What's your name?" she asked.

"Danno. Nice to meet you, Riley." He did the little Japanese bow that had replaced the handshake.

"Danno? What kind of name is that?"

"My dad was a big *Hawaii Five-O* fan, and his favorite character was Danno, the sidekick. Like, 'Book him, Danno.'"

Riley had no idea what he was talking about.

Danno pulled out a joint and waved it. "Break time. Want some? Employees get the best shit."

"Go ahead. I never smoke that way anymore. I'm strictly a vape girl. It's much safer."

Danno fired-up his joint and plopped down on the curb. Riley pulled out her vape pen, screwed in one of the cartridges, and the two sat three feet apart with the gate between them.

"How long does it take someone to die once they get it?" she asked, as the delicious vapor filled her lungs.

"Depends. Some go quickly, within a few days. With others, it can take a week or two."

Not long, Riley thought. *It seems like a humane way to go.*

Randall's uncle had died of kidney cancer, in agony for the last year of his life, and Randall always commented that he wanted to die fast.

"Do you think you could get any of the old masks?" Riley blurted, struck with a sudden thought that both thrilled and terrified her.

"Old masks?" Danno asked in confusion. "I can get you new ones. I know they're hard to come by right now, but they give them to us at work, and there are always extras."

"No, I mean an infected mask. With the virus still on it. One a patient wore."

"Jesus, why would you want that?" Danno asked. "It's really contagious."

Exactly, Riley thought, as she formulated a lie. "I'm a doctor, and I thought as long as I'm cooped up, I might as well take a crack at finding a cure."

"Wow, a doctor," Danno said in surprise. "No offense, but I wouldn't have guessed that.

Riley was prepared to be angry. "Why is that?"

"You're so fucking hot. I've never seen a doctor as beautiful as you."

Riley smiled. "So, can you get me a mask?"

"If you're doing research, wouldn't the government just give you some of the virus?"

The guy had more brainpower than she'd anticipated. "You know how the government is. Everything takes months. The big labs get all the support. I can't wait. I'd like to get to work right away."

"Cool," Danno said, thinking this might be karma calling. He'd made so many mistakes over the last year, but if he could help Riley cure Covid, it might even the scales a bit. "I guess I could get one. I still deliver pot to Moonlight."

"Great. Get an infected mask and put it into a Ziploc bag. I'll make it worth your while." She smiled.

Danno considered what that might mean. "Sure."

"Tomorrow afternoon, at three, you should park on the street." That was when Randall had his daily one-hour conference Zoom. Riley pointed to her right. "Walk through those trees, and you'll see a pool house. I'll be waiting. Of course, I might have just gotten out of the hot tub, so I hope it's okay if I'm not really dressed."

Danno couldn't believe his luck.

~

THE NEXT DAY, RILEY watched Danno sneak through the trees toward the pool bungalow. He had abandoned the astronaut's uniform for jeans and a T-shirt, and she was excited to discover his slim, muscled physique. She was wearing her best ViX Paula Hermanny black chain bikini and stopped to admire her firm ass in a mirror.

"Delivery for Riley." Danno tapped on the door, and then muttered, "Holy shit," as she opened it wide. He held a plastic bag in each hand. "You look incredible."

"You got them?" she asked.

"Just picked them up," Danno said proudly. "I deliver pot to a friend that works in the kitchen at Moonlight, and she got one of the nasty masks before it went into the incinerator. It belonged to Mrs. Neuman. She was ninety-two and really frail, but she was still pretty active when I was working there. Nice lady." Danno nodded sadly, voice dropping. "My friend was pretty confused by why I wanted it, but when I offered her five free Willie Nelson pre-rolls, she was happy to accommodate us." He held his right hand out. "This is the infected mask. Be careful with it." Riley set it on the counter. "And here's a clean one. A little present from Speedy Weedy. N95, the best you can buy, and right now, almost impossible to find unless you are doing essential work like me." he said, handing her the bag from his left hand. "Like I said, pot dealers get the best shit."

"Thanks," Riley said as she put it next to the other mask. "You want a beer? Wine?" She pointed at the open bottle of sauvignon blanc in an ice bucket.

"Sure, whatever you're having."

Riley poured him a glass and pointed toward the couch as she pulled out her vape pen.

"Your place is amazing," he said. "You must be a really good doctor."

She had the pleasant sense that she didn't need to lie to Danno. He seemed more like the kind of people she had grown up with. Since she'd married Randall, she always felt like a foreigner—the low-class chick that snuck into his hoity-toity world—which was its own kind of loneliness. "I was kidding about that," Riley said. "I'm not really a doctor. I needed the mask for something else. Don't ask."

"Okay. So what do you do?"

It was the question Riley hated, and for once, she decided to be honest. "I guess you could say I marry well. That probably makes me sound awful."

Danno shook his head. "I think it makes you sound smart. If I find a rich lady who wants to sweep me away to a mansion, you can bet I'll go for it. Hell, I'd marry Granny Clampett. Or Betty White. She seems fun."

Riley laughed. "You two would make a beautiful couple. Let me guess. You didn't grow up rich?"

"Far from it," Danno said. "I was raised in Sacramento. Dad was a security guard at the Capital—when he was sober. He caught me smoking pot when I was sixteen and gave me a major beating, which wasn't the first. Mom just watched and said I deserved it, so I said screw you to both and headed out. Been on my own since." He stopped to light a joint. "Hasn't been bad. Traveled a lot. I was a Juggalo for a year and followed the band around. It's been easy to find work. I'm a very friendly dude, though a bit of a stoner. I've become a pretty good surfer."

"A Juggalo! I didn't know they really existed."

"Insane Clown Posse is the shit," Danno said. "I'll take you to a concert sometime. You'll love it. What's your story?"

"Well, since we're talking music, you ever hear an old song called 'Fancy'? Bobbie Gentry sang it."

"Nope. And who the fuck is Bobbie Gentry?"

"Wow, you need to expand your musical knowledge past guys who dress like clowns. She's a great singer-songwriter from the sixties. Hot, too. Incredible hair. 'Fancy' is about this really poor teenage girl who gets turned out by her mother. The mom is dying and has another baby to support. Her husband takes off, and she's desperate, so she buys her daughter a sexy red dress and tells her to go turn tricks. The girl ends up marrying a rich guy and living in a penthouse."

"Sounds like a happy tune," Danno said. "I think I'll stick with the Posse. Is that what happened to you? Mom turn you out?"

"No, my mother was too busy scoring pills to spend time thinking about how to help me. She started taking Oxy when she hurt her back, and that was all she wrote. She ended up looking like an extra from *The Walking Dead*. Dear old dad didn't pay child support and was a little too handsy for my taste, so I turned myself out. Left home like you. Moved from Colorado to LA to Seattle: stripping, taking odd jobs, sometimes turning tricks. Met my husband in Seattle when I was working as a hostess at the Fairmont. Did some double duty there. Of course, he doesn't know much about my past. He thinks both my parents passed away, and I had a long career in hospitality." Riley giggled. "He just doesn't know how hospitable I was. Rich dudes don't want to marry women that make money from sex, though they're okay paying for it."

"It's a lot easier to grow up rich than it is to be poor and figure out how to survive. We're the tough ones. Here's to surviving." Danno held out his glass in a toast.

Riley smiled and clinked. "To the survivors."

"How's it going with Daddy Warbucks?" Danno asked.

"I can't stand the sight or smell of him. I avoid him as much as possible. Other than that, it's great."

"Sounds like a match made in hell. He's a major douche, huh?"

Riley hesitated. "Actually, no. Randall's a good guy. He treats me well. Always buys me presents. Tells me how much he loves me all the time. Last night he made this fabulous dinner. He knows I like lobster, so he had some flown in from Maine. Candles, wine, the whole thing."

"Sounds great."

"It was, but then I screwed it up. I found some reason to get irritated with him. Jumped up in the middle of the meal and stormed out. Spilled wine all over the table."

"What's the problem? Is he a cheater?"

Riley shook her head. "No, I'm the cheater in the family. Randall's pretty much the only one I don't fuck."

"I don't get it," Danno said. "Great guy. He's faithful and adores you. Why do you hate him?"

Riley realized she didn't know the answer. "I don't know. Daddy or anger issues. Maybe I'm just a stone-cold bitch. He makes me feel like a fraud. He disgusts me because I know he could do so much better than me, and it pisses me off he's so weak. It's hard to respect someone who could love someone like me." She took another deep toke off her vape. "Maybe he's not the one I really hate."

"Whew. That's some heavy psychological stuff," Danno said. "Might want to see someone to work through those issues. Most people would be thrilled to have someone wonderful love them and live in a place like this."

"Yeah, I'm a lot shittier than most people," Riley said, staring at the mask on the counter, now feeling hollow.

"Maybe you shouldn't be so hard on yourself," Danno said. "You're beautiful and smart. You had to do some tough things to survive. Seems like you're just working through some shit, but you've survived. You should be proud of yourself."

"Proud?" Riley snorted. "You're sweet." She retreated to on oversized rattan chair, puffing on her vape pen. "Come get your reward," she said mechanically, as she spread her legs and pointed at her crotch, feeling as if she was inhabiting someone else's body.

Later that night after she'd finished exercising in the gym, Riley discovered Randall in the kitchen stirring a pot of marinara sauce. "Hope you're in the mood for Italian," he said. "I'm making the veal you love so much."

"You're unbelievable," she said, shaking her head. "How can you be so nice to me?"

"How can I be nice to the woman I love?" Randall laughed.

"Seriously, I was such a bitch last night," Riley said. "Actually, I'm a nightmare most of the time. You don't deserve it."

"Wait a minute. Who are you? Where's my wife?" he joked. "You can't be Riley. She would never apologize."

"I didn't apologize. I said you could do better. If I were you, I'd smack the hell out of me, then kick me out."

Randall set down the spoon and pulled Riley into his arms. She initially pushed back, but finally relaxed into his embrace. "Riley, I just wish you could see the woman I see when I look at you."

After dinner, Riley retreated to the bungalow to retrieve her vape pen. Randall often chastised her for smoking it. "Read the news," he would urge. "People are getting sick from vaping. You never know what kind of chemicals they put in that oil." After the beautiful meal he had prepared, she didn't want to argue with him, and she also needed some alone time. She'd started to cry when he hugged her and felt ashamed for showing weakness. She poured another glass of wine and picked up the pen from the coffee table, sucking-in deeply. She closed her eyes and tilted her head upward as the vapor filled her lungs, sending a pleasant vibration through her body. She was a little drunk from dinner and the afternoon's festivities, and stumbled backward a step, grabbing the countertop for support. She felt sore and damp between her legs, and when she looked over at the rattan chair and recalled the afternoon, she was filled with an unfamiliar shame.

The mask in the plastic bag sat a foot away, and she fingered it, thinking about the old lady who had died wearing it. She couldn't imagine living into her nineties. In fact, she was surprised she had made it to her thirties. She'd imagined life would be short and hard, like navigating a minefield, knowing every step could be your last. Living that way meant grabbing any pleasure you could find, without regard for others. Love was synonymous with disappointment. It made you sloppy and silly, and ultimately just amplified pain.

She took another deep toke and refilled her glass, now feeling the not-unpleasant sensation of spinning. The lights from the pool filtered in blue waves against the glass on the door. She couldn't believe she'd thought about hurting Randall. She was progressing from angry and selfish to dangerous. She opened the plastic bag and examined the mask, turning it over and over. *Hours earlier it had covered a dead woman's face. Had the woman's last breath gone into the fabric? What was she thinking when she knew she was about to die?*

She pulled it to her face, breathing in deeply, wondering if she could smell death. She attached the strap around her head to secure the mask, then walked out to the pool, staring down into the water. If she fell in, she wouldn't fight it. She'd lie face down, her final gasp going through the wet mask, then her body would sink to the bottom. *That might be a beautiful way to go*, she thought. *My body drifting through water. Two last breaths going through the mask as my lungs fill with wet warmth.*

~

SHORTLY AFTER MIDNIGHT, RANDALL found his wife passed out in a chair by the pool. He was confused by the fact she was wearing a mask, but when he discovered the vape pen and empty wine bottle on the counter, he assumed she had gotten very drunk and high and probably did not know what she was doing. He carried her back to the bedroom, stopping once on the lawn when she began to vomit. Cleaning her up, he forced her to drink a glass of water and take two Advil, counseling her it would help with tomorrow's inevitable hangover, before retreating to a spare bedroom.

Then next morning, as predicted, Riley was sallow and in pain. He brought her toast and tea, which she refused. "Just leave me alone," she yelled, an order she repeated every time he looked in on her that day. Later that night, he watched his wife stumble into the kitchen. "Help," she garbled. "I can't breathe. I feel like I'm drowning."

He carried her into the car for the ten-minute drive to the hospital, but "hospital" was an overstatement; it was more a clinic for the minor ailments typical in a beach community. A lone doctor treated surfing accidents, dog bites, and STDs. They were not equipped to handle the influx of Corona patients that were streaming into the building, and Randall sat with her for two hours in an examination room before they rolled her away for treatment.

The next morning, Doctor Ving Ghupta, clad in an L.L. Bean rain suit, a sun buff encircling his head, found Randall sprawled across lime plastic chairs in the waiting room. This was the most dreaded part of his profession, that he had unfortunately gained a lot of practice at over the last few weeks. "I'm so sorry, but she didn't make it."

Randall jumped up and stared at him in amazement. "What are you talking about? She's only thirty-three-years old. Young people don't die of Covid."

"That's normally true," the doctor said, "but her lungs were a mess. They looked like organs you'd find on an eighty-year-old. I assume she was a heavy smoker?"

Randall buried his face in his hands, visualizing Riley with the damn vape pen stuck in her mouth. "You should try a little," she'd say, waving it toward him. "It's delicious. Dreamy McPotsy."

Verse III

A SMALL PRICE TO PAY FOR YO-YO MA

Stan McGreevy was a legend in Santa Pulmo. For over forty years, he had been one of the most popular teachers at Santa Pulmo High, where he taught music and directed the school band. Twenty-three of his students went on to enjoy significant musical careers, including the drummer for Stone Temple Pilots, five members of internationally renowned orchestras, backup singers for Paul Anka and Weird Al Yankovic, and a member of the *Jersey Boys*' traveling cast. In 1999, under Mr. McGreevy's leadership, the Santa Pulmo High Marching Band was named best in the nation and played at the Rose Bowl. The plumed shako that Mr. McGreevy wore that day while leading the band as drum major held a prime place in the school trophy case.

Mr. McGreevy could be demanding. His face would bunch in crimson agony as he guided cacophonous students through difficult Debussy or Vivaldi passages. However, he managed to temper musical passion with compassion and wisdom—the teacher kids turned to when they sought advice or needed to unload distressing secrets. He counseled teenagers on subjects ranging from abortion to tattoo removal. When Carl Taggert announced he was gay and was promptly ejected from his house, he took up residence in Mr. McGreevy's attic while he finished high school. When Lanny Williams' father lost his job, Stan pulled a few strings to get him hired in the high school maintenance department.

Jessie Burdett had particular affection for the man. In 1984, during her senior year of high school, he organized a concert in the park to raise funds to send her to Los Angeles for an audition for *Star Search*. Jessie had dreams of one day performing as the opening act for her idol Cyndi Lauper and had prepared a stirring rendition of "Time After Time," which earned her a slot on the show. Jessie sang her heart out but lost to an impish twelve-year-old doing a disturbingly sexy interpretation of Madonna's "Material Girl." Still, Ed McMahon took Jessie to lunch, and she met Rosie O'Donnell and Sawyer Brown. Even though she ultimately abandoned her musical dreams to open a bookstore in Santa Pulmo, she credited Mr. McGreevy with giving her a brief glimpse into a dream world most people never get to experience.

The previous February, when Mr. McGreevy suffered a massive stroke while conducting Puccini's "Nessun Dorma," the community came together in support. Mrs. McGreevy had passed away the previous year, and the only option was to house Mr. McGreevy in Moonlight Cove. Money was raised to upgrade him to a private suite, and former students became frequent visitors to their old mentor. Unfortunately, it was hard to gauge Mr. McGreevy's reaction, as his face frozen into a Muncian scowl.

All contact to the outside world was cut-off when Corona struck Moonlight Cove, killing many of the residents and isolating the rest. Friends were terrified for Mr. McGreevy, but he somehow managed to avoid contracting the virus, and he was instead relegated to solitary confinement.

Jessie Burdett came up with the idea for the concert. Forced by the pandemic to close her bookstore, she found herself with a lot of free time and an existential need to perform community service. She contacted the members of her old high school band, Jessie and the J Girls, to suggest they put the group back together. With Jessie singing lead, Deb Weekley on guitar, Jill Taylor on drums, and Pam Standley on bass, the group attempted to rekindle rock magic while rehearsing at a safe distance in Deb's backyard. Even the ladies would admit their recreations of Pat Benatar, The Bangles, and Go-Go's classics left a lot to be desired, but they figured it might bring a little pleasure to Mr. McGreevy and the Moonlight Cove residents; so on a Saturday afternoon, they set-up on the lawn, covid-spaced, in front of Mr. McGreevy's room.

The residents initially looked confused and annoyed as Jessie and the band belted out "Hit Me With Your Best Shot" and "Love is a Battlefield," but warmed when they got to "Manic Monday" and "We've Got The Beat." It was difficult to judge if Mr. McGreevy enjoyed the performance, though he continued to stare out his window for the entire hour.

Word of the concert spread through the community, and Jessie received a call from an old classmate, Robert Cook. Robert and Jessie had been in the marching band together, and Robert now taught musical theory at Santa Pulmo State University. "I'm thinking of putting together a string quartet to play for Mr. McGreevy and the residents."

"I love it," Jessie said. She knew that Mr. McGreevy was much more a fan of Bach than The Bangles.

That weekend, she sat on the hood of her car in the Moonlight Cove parking lot, listening to Robert and the group perform Schubert's "Death and the Maiden." Mr. McGreevy's window was open, and he stared at the musicians, his head shaking back and forth.

The performances were so successful that they decided to make them a regular Saturday event. The *Santa Pulmo Explorer* did a cover story on the event, which was picked up by the newswires, the press looking for any hint of good news. "It's incredible," Jose, the manager of the retirement home exclaimed to the reporter. "It gives residents hope and something to look forward to."

Jessie was acknowledged as the founder of the Moonlight Cove concert series, as they were now called. A couple weeks later, she received a strange and thrilling email:

Read about the great work you are doing for Moonlight Cove. I'll be passing through town and would be glad to give a short performance. All my best, Yo-Yo Ma.

Jessie assumed it was a joke. She checked the email address: YYMa@gmail.com. Is it possible, she wondered? She forwarded it to Robert, asking if this could be real.

Unfortunately, I am not personally acquainted with Mr. Ma. Seems dubious, but it can't hurt to explore.

Assuming it was some kind of financial scam—he would probably ask her to forward money to some offshore account—Jessie replied, *Thanks so much for your offer, and we would love to have you perform, but we don't have a budget to host celebrity talent.*

You misunderstand, YYMa@gmail.com replied. *No need for compensation. I'd be happy to stop by Saturday and play for a few minutes. My only request is a small cooler of Pabst Blue Ribbon beer. I enjoy a cold one on weekend afternoons.*

It made no sense. When she discussed it with Robert, he suggested they extend the invitation. "What have we got to lose? I'm curious to see who shows up. It's worth a six pack just to see what happens."

YYMa@gmail.com told Jessie to expect him promptly at three. *Don't forget the beer,* he reminded her. Robert and Jessie kept the visitor secret, afraid of the embarrassment if it turned out to be a hoax. On Saturday, a small crowd gathered at Moonlight Cove, expecting the usual concert. By regulation, they were not supposed to leave their cars, but a few people climbed onto the roofs of their vehicles.

The Moonlight Cove residents pulled chairs to their windows, awaiting the afternoon entertainment. Robert's group was ready to play, assuming there was no way in hell Yo-Yo Ma was coming.

Jessie and Robert, standing apart on the lawn, watched a dented Jeep pull in. A sixty- something-year-old masked Asian man, dressed in cargo shorts and a T-shirt emblazoned with I LISTEN TO DEAD PEOPLE, hustled toward them, followed by a young woman with purple-streaked hair. Her face was covered with a sun buff, and she was texting while she walked. "Are you Jessie?" she yelled.

Jessie turned to Robert, throwing a "Is it possible it's him" look. Robert shook his head with an "I don't know" gesture.

Jessie yelled a greeting, and the man stopped ten feet away and bowed in the Corona greeting. "Nice to meet you. I'm Yo-Yo. Want me to play right there?" he pointed at a stool set in the center of the lawn.

Jessie nodded in amazement. "Yes. Thanks so much for coming."

"Did you bring the beer?"

Jessie pointed at the small cooler sitting a few feet away.

"Wonderful," the man replied, clapping his hands. "It's a perfect day for music and a brew, isn't it?" His eyes curled in what she assumed was a smile. The purple-haired woman walked forward, pulled a disinfectant wipe out of her purse, cleaned the handle, removed a beer, wiped the top before popping it, and handed it to the man before opening one for herself. They pulled up their masks to take sips.

"Will play for beer," the man laughed. "Ever see a homeless guy with a sign like that?"

Jessie smiled and nodded, still unsure what was happening.

"Can I borrow a cello?"

"You don't want to play your own instrument?" Robert asked in amazement.

"We don't carry Petunia around in that old thing," the man motioned at the Jeep. "We're camping. It's too rough on an instrument."

Robert yelled at one of the quartet members, who brought over a cello and set it next to the stool. The woman pulled out another wipe, cleansed the stool and neck of the instrument, and nodded at the man before she returned to the Jeep.

"I was thinking 'Cello Suite No. 1 in G Major' to begin," he said.

Jessie and Robert blankly nodded.

He sat on the stool and took up the instrument and bow. The crowd leaned forward, realizing they were experiencing something special. Robert closed his eyes, head back, drinking in the music. At one point, he looked at Jessie and mouthed, "Oh my God."

He played for forty-five minutes, rising to thunderous applause, the Moonlight Cove residents screaming "bravo" out their windows. Mr. McGreevy's head bobbed up and down as he grunted, "Yo-Yo, Yo-Yo."

The man bowed and waved.

"Incredible," Jessie said, "Thank you so much." Robert seemed too awestruck to say anything.

"Happy to do it," he said. "Thanks for the PBR," he said, leaning down to pick up the cooler. "Sorry, but we need to run."

The purple-haired girl hustled toward them. "Hate to ask, but would you happen to have a few bucks for gas?"

Jessie and Robert exchanged confused glances, and Robert pulled out his wallet. "I have sixty," he said, setting the bills on the grass and backing up.

"Thanks," she said.

As the Jeep rolled out, Robert followed Jessie back to her car. "So, it really was him?" Robert asked. "What do you think? Yo-Yo-fucking-Ma?"

Jessie noticed her car door was ajar and looked inside. The glove box had been rifled, contents strewn all over the seats and floor. "I don't know, but I think Yo-Yo's girlfriend stole my sunglasses and four bucks' worth of quarters."

"A small price to pay for Yo-Yo Ma," concluded Robert.

Verse IV

YABBA DABBA DOOM

DANNO SAT IN FRONT of his computer and logged into Ticketmaster, twitchy as the clock ticked down. In four minutes and fifty-nine seconds—fifty-eight, fifty-seven—passes would go on sale for Yabba Dabba Doo, the two-day music festival Danno anticipated would be his generation's Woodstock, a life-altering experience.

A proud Juggalo, Danno would pay the price of admission just to see the headliner, Insane Clown Posse. But the weekend lineup also included Limp Bizkit, Assjack, Twiztid, and Rob Zombie.

Danno had been planning to attend the event for months. Right after his shift ended at Moonlight Cove on Thursday, he and Pugs would make the five-hour-drive to snag a primo camping spot. Pugs normally ridiculed the whole Juggalo thing, preferring Drake or Kanye—Danno even discovered him listening to Taylor Swift in a shameful episode he continued to harass him about—but Danno promised him "oodles of pussy" and a "totally fucked-up weekend."

Yabba Dabba Doo was being staged at the defunct Starlight Drive-in Theater outside of Reno—rechristened Bedrock for the festival—the parking spots converted into camping spaces. Danno planned to pitch his tent near the front. He'd purchased a used Aerobed on eBay to place under his sleeping bag to protect from rashes. He packed a propane grill to cook his favorite Top Ramen but anticipated buying most of his meals from the snack bar, which featured a special themed menu: brontosaurus burgers, Wilma fries, Bam Bam cookies, spiked Cactus Coola, and Busch beer.

A bandstand was erected at the front of the drive-in, and cameras would project the performers onto the screen. *Danno imagined a twenty-foot-tall Shaggy 2 Dope, in full Clown Posse regalia, belting out Hokus Pokus.*

But there would be more to this experience than music. The organizers planned a wide variety of events around the Flintstone theme. Danno had stocked-up on Molly in anticipation of the Barney and Betty love-in, in which participants were encouraged to slather mud on each other's nude bodies. The website warned there were no showers, so they would have to rinse with a hose, but still.

On Thursday morning, he reminded his boss at Moonlight Cove he was taking a vacation day. "I can't believe you're going to a concert now," Jose commented. "Seems dangerous."

"Why?" asked Danno.

"The Corona virus. That shit's real, dude."

"Ha," said Danno. "Maybe if you're eighty. If you're young, the worst you get is a little cold."

Jose shook his head. "I'm surprised they're even allowing it. They say everything is closing down in the next day or two."

"It's in Nevada. Nothing ever closes."

Jose waved a hand. "I'm not your mother. Knock yourself out. Drive drunk. Have unprotected sex with a Haitian hooker. I don't give a fuck. Just don't be late for work on Monday."

Jose resembled a strip club bouncer more than the manager of a retirement home. The owners were primarily concerned with cost containment so they could cash in on the meager Medicare payments, and accordingly, pay scales and employment standards were low. Jose had worked there for five years, originally placed via a prison release program. Luckily for Danno, Jose hadn't required a background check when he hired him, just happy to find a Caucasian that didn't mind doing the job, as many of the residents suffered racist paranoia, accusing any person of color of theft or worse.

Danno nodded. "See you Monday, boss."

On the way out, he stopped to see Stanley Amos, his favorite resident. "How are you feeling today, Colonel?" he asked with a little salute. Stanley was retired Army and, on days when reality was fleeting, sometimes believed Moonlight Cove was Fort Bragg, Danno his Adjutant.

"I was tip-top until I saw you. You're a sorry excuse for a soldier," he barked. "Filthy uniform, and you need a haircut. Get your shit together, Lieutenant."

Danno's mouth dropped open. "Uh, sorry, Colonel, I just…"

"Ha," Stanley laughed. "Got you. Don't worry, Danno. I know where I am today. Here in paradise with all the other old farts eating oatmeal and watching *Matlock*."

Danno nodded, relieved. "Well, I just wanted to let you know I'm going to be gone a few days. Heading to Nevada for a concert."

"A concert? Hell, since Sinatra and Dino died, there's nobody worth going to Nevada to see," Stanley said. "Hope you're not going all that way to see that twiggy Celine Dion. Voice like a smoke alarm." He squinted at Danno and lowered his voice. "You can tell me the truth. We're all men here. You going there to do a little whoring? Spending a weekend at The Bunny Ranch?"

Danno laughed. "No, Stanley, I'm really going to a concert, and not Celine Dion. I just wanted to make sure you are in good shape and see if you needed anything. I don't want you to forget to take your Zestril."

"I will," Stanley said, annoyed. "And don't forget your pills. You're going to need a big bottle of Viagra, even at your age, if you're going to spend the whole weekend at the Ranch. Those girls will ride you like a horny palomino."

"Sure, Stanley," Danno said. "I'll see you in a few days."

"Ask for Lydia," Stanley yelled as Danno walked away. "Big girl, but she's got a miracle cootchie. And wrap your rascal."

Yabba Dabba Doo exceeded all expectations, aside from the terrible groin rash he woke up with after the Barney and Betty love-in. He suspected the mud wasn't hygienic and rolling around on dirty blacktop had left marks. But the event had even been a moneymaker. He'd brought seventy-five pre-rolled joints that he sold for ten bucks per, which paid for his ticket.

He arrived back at his apartment at two a.m. Monday morning. Before slumping off to a shower and bed, he checked the work schedule taped to the refrigerator. With a loud, "Oh fuck," he realized he was booked for an early shift in a few hours. Given Jose's warning, he needed to show up, and he slumped into bed, barely able to lift himself up when the alarm rang at five.

The next day was agony. "Shouldn't mix molly, hash, coke, and Cactus Coola," he surmised, as he trudged through Moonlight Cove, emptying residents' bedpans, pushing hampers of sheets to the laundry, and helping elderly residents into the cafeteria. On his break, he stumbled to the far end of the parking lot to suck down a joint, which eased the pain a bit.

Danno certainly didn't enjoy soiled Depends and the general odor of decay that permeated the workplace, though he did like his job. He'd had a troubled relationship with his father and craved attention from older males. He loved hearing war stories from the old men, especially Stanley's World War II tales. At 101, Stanley was the oldest member of the Moonlight Cove community, and Danno would often spend his lunch hour with him, fascinated by his adventures in Europe fighting the Nazis.

"Joined the army to kick some ass and get some ass," Stanley would announce, often to the hostile stares of other residents. When he wasn't in battle, Stanley had devoted most of his time to pursuing women attracted to men in uniform—which he claimed was a high percentage of the female population. Danno wasn't sure if he should believe all of Stanley's raunchy stories but took some satisfaction in the fact that a centenarian could be so damn horny.

Danno had also built a lucrative side hustle as the official pot dealer to the retirement home—throwing Jose ten percent—amazed to discover how many of these oldsters were total heads. He was careful to keep the prices reasonable, more interested in providing a public service to the residents than acting like a drug dealer.

On Tuesday he woke up feeling even worse, throat swollen, hacking a dry cough. He considered calling in sick but didn't want to push his luck, given he'd just been on vacation. He stumbled through the day, sweating profusely as a fever set in. Wednesday was even worse, and after lunch Jose pulled him aside.

"Get the fuck out of here," he instructed. "Some of the residents are complaining you're coughing on them."

That night Pugs called. "Dude, I am super ill," he told Danno.

"Me, too. I can barely breathe."

"Dude, do you think we have it?" Pugs asked.

"You think?"

"Did you see the news?" Pugs said. "People are super pissed off about Yabba Dabba Doo. They said it created a Corona hot spot. Eighty cases so far and growing. I read online that DJ Vag and Beans Del Monte have it."

Danno's stomach bottomed. He had assumed it was just a hangover. "I heard it's almost impossible for young people to catch it."

"Hopefully you're right," Pugs said. "I guess Beans *is* pretty old. Dude's got to be at least thirty-five."

Four days later when he returned to work, Danno was blocked from pulling into the parking lot at Moonlight Cove by a line of hearses and ambulances. Men in hazmat suits were rolling bodies out a side door. Jose was standing outside, clad in a plastic jumpsuit and mask, shifting from leg to leg. Danno thought he looked coked-up.

"What's happening?" Danno asked.

"Half the residents have the virus. Four of them died last night. We can't keep up."

"Oh, my God. Who died?"

Jose rattled off names, ending with Stanley Amos.

"Jesus," Danno said, as he remembered their last lunch, Danno coughing while Stanley ate his soup.

"I hope you weren't the one that infected this place," Jose said. "You and your goddamn Fred Flintstone concert."

"Jesus, Jose, I don't think…"

"No, you *don't* think," Jose interrupted, "hanging out with thousands of people when there's a plague."

"You can't be sure it was me. A lot of people are sick. I don't know if I even had Corona. I think I just had a hangover. Somebody else could have brought it in. Families have been coming in and out."

"Maybe, maybe not," Jose said bitterly. "In any case, we must keep this quiet. If people think you infected everyone, and I let you do it, we'd both be in trouble. So, you're fired. We don't need as many orderlies now since you thinned the population, and I don't want you around if people start asking questions. If you ever tell anyone you were sick and I knew about it, or if you ever mention our little deal, I will deny everything, and I will find you in the middle of the night and collapse your pinhead skull with a hammer. Get lost."

Danno slumped in a daze to his car. *Did he kill Stanley and the others?* Returning to his apartment, he drank a beer, smoked two bowls, and crawled into bed in a fetal position. He stayed there for hours, dreaming in a hash haze, Stanley floating in front of him, hacking violently, yelling in-between coughs, "I survived the Depression, the Nazis, North Korea, Vietnam, and a dozen cases of the clap. But not you. Thanks for killing me, kid."

At midnight, he poured a bowl of cereal and grabbed his laptop to begin researching Covid. Yabba Dabba Doo was a national story. Rachel Maddow chastised the gathering, calling the attendees Yabba Dabba Dopes. Danno was no mathematician, but he began trying to calculate the odds he had infected the home, which drew him into a deeper depression.

Looking for any relief, he dug into right-wing websites that took a different perspective on the disease: It's just the flu. It's a Chinese bio attack. It's fake news the Democrats are spreading. Multiple explanations that would clear him.

None of the ideas offered him comfort, since it didn't explain the dead bodies at Moonlight Cove, but then he stumbled across a blog post from TRUAMERICANPATRIOT, which clarified that Covid was really a deep state plot to kill Trump voters. *That's why it's hitting the elderly. George Soros, Hillary, and the rest of the deep state know that people over sixty have a better understanding of the world, and therefore are Trump supporters. The only ones that hate Trump more than the deep state are the Chinese, because Trump has devastated their economy. China developed Covid specifically to kill older people, and agents from the deep state are spreading it among elderly populations to murder Trump voters before the election. Then, the deep state will work with the Chinese to turn America into a communist extension of China, with Obama put back in place as the American dictator.*

Initially, it sounded crazy to Danno, but TRUAMERICANPATRIOT was persuasive, citing multiple sources like @FORMERCIAGUY, @REALNAVYSEAL, and other covert experts who had first-hand knowledge of the Chinese plot. Danno had never been political and didn't have a strong opinion on Trump. He had watched an old episode of *The Celebrity Apprentice*, but only because he was a Meatloaf fan, and recalled thinking Trump was stiff and doughy—not the kind of guy you'd share a joint with—and otherwise gave him little thought. However, he was aware a lot of people hated the president, and it didn't seem impossible that there would be a plot to unseat him.

Danno decided to contact TRUAMERICANPATRIOT, though he doubted someone that important would have time to respond. He sent an email, detailing his fears he had contracted the virus at Yabba Dabba Doo and spread it to Moonlight Cove. Much to his surprise, he had a response within sixty seconds. *This isn't your fault. The Chinese and deep state are insidious. Like the rest of America, you were a victim of a sneak attack, just like Pearl Harbor.*

TRUAMERICANPATRIOT told Danno that his team was investigating the Yabba Dabba Doo incident. The news was now claiming over two hundred people had been infected. *We doubt those numbers and think the left-wing press is lying to make the President look bad. If there was an outbreak, it was likely spread by the Chinese,* he said. *Do you remember encountering any Chinese at the concert?*

Danno recalled an episode at the snack bar. He was at the condiment counter, slathering his brontosaurus burger with sriracha, when the Asian girl next to him commented, "Wow, you really like it spicy." She had reached across his food to grab the mustard. Perhaps she had dropped something on his meal. At the time, Danno thought she was interested in hooking-up, and he threw a couple of his best lines at her, but she didn't respond.

Could be, if you really were infected. TRUAMERICANPATRIOT replied when Danno related the encounter. *If so, you were a victim.*

Danno felt enormous relief. He and TRUAMERICANPATRIOT continued emailing for another hour, with Danno agreeing to become a Patriot Marketing Associate and sell the special zinc tablets—Patriot Pills—and the American Envirosanitizer Blu Light advertised on TRUAMERICANPATRIOT'S site. He instructed Danno on how to sanitize his apartment with the light and told him to take the Patriot Pills daily.

The tab for the lights and pills came to nineteen hundred dollars—an expense Danno could ill-afford given he was unemployed, but TRUAMERICANPATRIOT assured him it was a short-term investment that would pay big dividends. *You can do this full-time now that you're not working,* TRUAMERICANPATRIOT encouraged him. *You'll make a lot of money, while also protecting people. We need to get everyone using these products to stay healthy during the war.* Still harboring guilt over Moonlight Cove, Danno felt good about becoming a soldier in the fight against the Chinese Deep State virus. At five a.m., he finally signed off.

The next morning, overflowing with energy, Danno banged on Pug's door. "Where's your laptop?" he yelled, barging into Pug's apartment. Pug, never a morning person, was wearing boxer shorts and a Santa Pulmo State University T-shirt, even though he had flunked out of the institution during his first semester. "Least I got a cool shirt," he would brag.

Danno excitedly showed him the website and related his conversations with TRUAMERICANPATRIOT. "Get out your credit card," he instructed Pugs. "You need to order this stuff."

Pugs had little interest in anything political, normally limiting his shopping to fast food, video games, curated online porn, and Red Bull—but he was fascinated by the Patriot Pills, which the site advertised as "effective prevention and treatment for Covid 19, Alzheimer's, and various forms of dementia."

"Do you think this shit really works?" he asked Danno.

"I don't think they could say that if it doesn't. A lot of people think that the pharmaceutical companies cover up all kinds of natural cures just to make money."

Pugs had seen his burgeoning Uber business evaporate due to Covid and had been racking his brain to come up with new employment that allowed similar flexibility. "This is it," he said to Danno, grabbing his wallet. "We're going to make a fortune."

~

Nine days later, Pugs and Danno, both wearing white lab coats purchased on Amazon, were standing in front of a rented canvas canopy they'd erected at the edge of Benjamin Franklin Park. Pugs found an old stethoscope that his mother—a retired nurse—had left in a medical kit and draped it around his neck. Danno had made up nametags for both of them, christening himself "Dr. Dan," and Pugs, "Professor Hanley."

"People will take us more seriously," he explained, sticking the nametag to his lapel even though he doubted anyone would possibly believe they had gone to college, much less med school.

They placed large signs on both sides of the canopy: PREVENT AND TREAT COVID. Card tables under the canopy were stacked with bottles of Patriot Pills, and an American Envirosantizer sat elevated on a white box with a sign that said, KILLS VIRUSES WITH PATENTED LIGHT. They priced the pills at $99.99 for a thirty-day supply, which afforded them a decent five hundred percent mark-up, and the light at $399.99, three times what they paid for the device.

Much to their surprise, a line quickly formed, with most people buying multiple bottles, and within an hour, they had sold out of lights. Danno had anticipated more questions and skepticism—which he was dreading—but the crowd was hungry for anything that resembled respite from the epidemic. They were down to their last three bottles when the police car pulled up.

Patrolwoman Kathy Best of the Santa Pulmo PD had received a report of a large gathering in the park, which was closed by the Governor's stay-at-home order. The crowd dissipated when she arrived, and Danno shoved the last bottles into his pocket.

"What's going on?" Officer Best asked.

"Nothing," Pugs said. "Just closing down." Danno watched him throw his famous smile. Pugs was a good-looking guy—girls said he resembled Zac Efron—and he could often charm his way out of trouble.

Officer Best looked at the sign. "You're selling a cure for Covid?"

"No," Pugs said, pulling out his iPhone. "We're just shooting a TikTok. Just a funny video. Maybe send it in to *The Daily Show*, that kind of thing."

Officer Best looked at him skeptically. "Well, the park's closed, and I could fine you for being here."

"Closed? Geez," Pugs said. "We didn't know. We'll pack up right away. I'm so sorry." He stepped closer to examine her nametag, but she backed up. "Is it Kathy?"

She snorted. "It's Officer Best. Just be out of here in five minutes, otherwise you'll be paying a big fine."

They quickly pulled down the displays, loaded them into the back of Pug's Kia Sportage, and drove back to Pug's apartment to count the money. "We cleared almost ten thousand dollars," Danno shrieked.

"That's just the beginning," Pugs said. "We need to restock and set up a route. We can hit all the towns in this area."

"Plus, think of all the lives we'll be saving," Danno said.

"Sure, that, too." Pugs laughed, assuming Danno was joking.

~

THEY HAD BOTH MAXED out their credit cards on the first order, so Danno asked TRUAMERICANPATRIOT if he could extend them terms on a ten-thousand-dollar order of Pills and Envirosanitizers, assuring him they would pay him back within a week.

It was by far the largest order in the history of TRUAMERICAN-PATRIOT, and the owner did not want to blow it, but sent a stern warning. *You have seven days to pay the balance, and if you don't, you can expect a visit from two of my associates, both former Mossad, to collect. Trust me, you don't want to meet them.*

Danno and Pugs purchased a larger canopy and invested in professionally made signs. Pug's uncle owned an auto body shop that was forced to close, and he bought their supply of paper painter's masks to add to the product line. "These look just like those N95 masks online. I paid my uncle fifty cents per mask. I think we can get ten bucks each," he told Danno. "I'm going to make a sign and call them N99 masks—even better than N95."

Danno wasn't comfortable lying, but he had read there was a mask shortage and figured they'd be doing a service by making them available. Even if they were expensive, it was impossible to put a price on health. He couldn't help but wonder if things would have turned out differently if people had worn masks at Moonlight Cove.

They set up their pop-up store in the parking lot of a strip mall near Costco. The businesses in the mall—which included a Chinese rub and tug, a tattoo parlor, and a discount tobacco store—were closed. Business was brisk, and a long line of buyers had formed when two police cars pulled into the lot.

Patrolwoman Kathy Best, flanked by two other officers, approached Danno and Pugs. "Making another video for *The Daily Show*?" she asked sarcastically.

"Okay, Kathy, you got us," Pugs said. "Actually, we're doing our part to help out during the pandemic. We're selling stuff that people really need."

"It's Officer Best," she answered, examining a bottle of the pills. "I don't suppose you have a business license and an essential services permit?"

"It's on our list to get as soon as we can, but we thought it was more urgent to get out all this lifesaving merchandise."

Officer Best inspected the Envirosanitizer. "You know that this is just an aquarium light, don't you? You can buy one in a pet store for around fifteen bucks."

"Jesus," Pugs turned to Danno. "TRUAMERICANPATRIOT is really ripping people off."

Officer Best pulled out her handcuffs and nodded at her partner. "We're going to arrest you for a whole bunch of violations. Probably more than I'm even thinking of right now. We need to figure out what the hell is in those pills you're selling. I hope they don't kill anyone, or you'll be facing a murder charge."

Murder? Danno grimaced. *Am I accidentally turning into a serial killer?*

"Kathy, c'mon. I'm sure we can work this out," Pugs said. "We're happy to shut it down. We just want to help people."

"It's Officer Best," she replied, snapping the cuffs hard around his wrists.

Bail was set at twenty-five hundred each, and their attorney required a three-thousand-dollar retainer, which ate up most of the profits from initial sales. The police impounded all the merchandise and cash. Luckily for Pugs and Danno, authorities determined the pills that supposedly cured Covid were rebottled Costco-branded zinc tablets, so at least they weren't charged with poisoning people. They both had big credit card payments due and no way to pay TRUAMERICANPATRIOT. Their case was deemed "non-essential" since the court was largely shutdown, which meant the hearing was months away, and their money and merch would stay locked away.

To compound matters, reporters and healthcare investigators were now harassing Danno. Word had gotten out that he might be patient zero of the Moonlight Cove pandemic, which had now claimed ten victims with many more on respirators. Danno moved out of his place in the middle of the night to take up residence on Pug's couch.

They woke up to an online story in the *Santa Pulmo Explorer* that featured a photo of a smiling Danno pushing an elderly woman in a wheelchair. He remembered the morning a relative had taken the picture a few months earlier. The caption said, OFFICIALS INVESTIGATING COVID SPREAD AT MOONLIGHT COVE.

"Wow, you're famous," Pugs said. "Even got the front page."

"Fuck you," Danno replied, fighting back tears. "I wish we'd never gone to that concert. Jesus, do you think I really might have infected those people? Killed Stanley and all the others?"

"That's ridiculous," Pug assured him. "It's a pandemic. They could have gotten it anywhere."

Danno looked down when his email pinged. *WHERE'S MY MONEY?* TRUAMERICANPATRIOT demanded, the email marked urgent. *IF I DON'T HAVE IT BY TOMORROW EXPECT A VISIT FROM THE MOSSAD.*

"I'm so screwed," Danno said. "And I might be a murderer,"

"Oh, cheer up," Pugs said, punching him in the arm. "It will all be okay. Hey, you know what I always say when things look darkest?"

"What?" Danno looked up at his friend.

"Yabba dabba doo," Pugs declared, breaking into a caveman dance.

Verse V
COVID COWBOY

I'M NOT HOMELESS, DESPITE how it appears. You see me lying prone in the concrete V where the freeway overpass intersects terra firma, a place not designed for human habitation. You make assumptions and rush to lock your car door at the sight of the zombie camp: the unwashed shuffling among shopping carts, makeshift tents, piled trash, bodies draped over tattered unloved couches. You assume one of the following:

1. Those disgusting, lazy loafers need to buck up and get a job.
2. Go back to your shit-hole country.
3. Those poor people—which leads to reasonable and sometimes correct assumptions about what brought us here.

Though you might have correctly profiled many professional can pickers, I want to clarify: you have me wrong. I am not a deranged vet running from the ghosts of my Afghan war victims. I am not on the street because fifteen years ago, perverted Uncle Tony or the gruff Monsignor from Holy Rosary stroked my pre-pubescent dick. I enjoy alcohol and a few tasty drugs of choice—I have special affection for pharmaceuticals in the hydrocodone bitartrate hydromorphone family—but I did not abandon civilization to pursue addictions that would strip me of humanity and my teeth.

I did experience all the traditional hallmarks of the nomadic, trailer-dwelling American family beset by income inequality:

a self-obsessed, alcoholic father who died young; a depressed, underemployed mother; and a rotation of public schools so mediocre it's amazing I don't read with a fifth grader's comprehension. However, I've been more fortunate than most, blessed with a solid brain and a level disposition—Mom used to joke I must have been switched at birth from a much smarter family—and I've never been one to indulge in self-pity. Instead, I've tried to conduct myself with dignity and a certain formality that I find comforting. I entered a new high school during my sophomore year and attempted to speak with an English accent, consulting ancient Alec Guinness movies for inspiration. Having watched so many people around me implode, I found the "stiff upper lipness" of the British inspirational. Unfortunately, my classmates soon discovered my real lineage, and I became "the freak that thinks he's James Bond."

A year ago, I was a fresh graduate of the University of Phoenix (*Arlington, Texas campus—the Harvard of the University of Phoenix empire*), working in the IT department at JCPenney, where I attempted to whittle away a student debt that exceeded my grandfather's lifetime savings.

The first kerfuffle…a misunderstanding with my girlfriend, Shelly. I had moved in with her three months earlier after a whirlwind romance that sprouted in the bar at Applebee's, and our relationship was progressing nicely. Until I made the big mistake.

After a hard day valiantly attempting to maintain a computer system last deemed state-of-the-art during the Clinton administration, I needed a cocktail and some sympathetic conversation. My coworker Cynthia shared my technical expertise and desire for libations, which led us to a back booth at The Tipsy Cow. Three rounds of happy hour margaritas later, Cynthia professed sexual fantasies so mesmerizing I lost control.

I'm not accustomed to being propositioned. My mom's dismal financial situation during my teen years did not allow for cosmetic dentistry, so I have the smile of a Dr. Seuss character. In clothes, you would probably describe me as skinny. Naked, I'm a doughy giraffe. No matter how hard I work out, my lanky frame remains covered with rolls of thick skin that make me look like a deflated Michelin Man sporting man boobs. My left testicle is the size of a Gigantes bean. I do not have a lot of experience in the carnal arts.

Unfortunately, on her way home, Shelly noticed my car in Tipsy's lot. When she peeked in the window, she was confronted with the distressing sight of Cynthia's head, mouth stuffed with cracked margarita-flavored ice, bobbing up and down like a buoy in a storm, a move she coyly called the "tequila blow." By the time I extricated myself from the position and returned to the apartment, Shelly had deposited my belongings in the parking lot and refused to unbolt the door. I couldn't blame her—it was a cad's move I still regret—and I transitioned from a comfy home in the Bellwether Studios to the decidedly less nurturing Staycation Inn.

Strike two occurred the following Friday, when my position at JCPenney was eliminated. America no longer values heritage, and I suspect James Cash Penney would roll in his grave if he knew his namesake had been destroyed by Bezos, the bald villain using the country as a dumping ground for Chinese bric-a-brac while clogging our alleys with logoed cardboard. Of course, you could rightly point out that the Penney's brand has devolved into the retailer that sells "as seen on TV" products and incontinence supplies to old folks piloting mobility scooters—the retail equivalent of an Oldsmobile parked at the end of an abandoned mall—but still, it was an American institution. The company gave me two weeks' severance, but the most disturbing part was when my boss pulled me aside.

"Don't list me as a reference," he said. "I'd have to be honest."

I am not well suited for corporate America. I have trouble keeping my opinions to myself, which is never welcome in a bureaucracy. Still, I did not anticipate difficulty obtaining new employment. I had graduated from an institution so revered they were allowed to run ads on *The Big Bang Theory*. However, right about that time, someone in China ate a bat burrito, and suddenly we were in the midst of a worldwide pandemic.

You might have read that the average American only has $400 in savings, which, in my case, inflated my net worth by a factor of four. Nobody was hiring. The Staycation Inn was unwilling to consider my pending unemployment benefits as collateral for lodging. I was without a home, *which is different from being homeless.*

A hundred and fifty years ago, men without homes headed west, and we called them explorers and cowboys. Nobody ever says, "I was reading a book about two homeless guys, Lewis and Clark." When you watch old westerns, you never say, "I saw a great movie last night starring John Wayne as a bum." John Wayne played cowboys. Men driven by circumstances and a restless and curious nature to explore the West, and perhaps make it a little better. Honorable men, but usually without lodging. Men like me, or at least the kind of man I aspire to be. A Covid Cowboy. Instead of plains and mountains, I opted to explore beach communities with favorable climates.

Initially, my six-month-old Kia Sportage provided transportation and housing as I headed west. Old-timey cowboys rode horses powered by millions of acres of free grass. I discovered my own endless font of no-cost fuel: siphoning gas from lonely cars idled by the pandemic. At night, I'd park in the back of Walmart lots, duck inside to use the restroom and clean up, and occasionally pilfer a few energy bars and packets of Applegate Black Forest ham and Tillamook cheese, feeling little guilt since I was stealing from the corporation that decimated small-town America.

I had made it to LA when Big Brother caught up. I was parked in Venice Beach, and when I returned, an African American gentleman with biceps the circumference of my waist was dragging the Kia onto the back of a flatbed. The Korean corporation had located my vehicle—perhaps notified when the pricey ticket attached to the wiper was filed—and since the payments were four months in arrears, they'd dispatched "Devon" to recover the car. Luckily, he was a big man with a big heart, and he allowed me to retrieve my scant belongings.

That placed me on the streets of LA, graduate school for the disenfranchised. Crooks, kooks, hustlers, addicts, and the truly down and out…they all roam the streets in their own little *Lord of the Flies—Hollywood Edition* reality show. I spent a couple of weeks sleeping in alleys and alcoves, engaged in long discussions with emaciated folks spouting conspiracy theories, and burglarizing cars for parking meter change, when it dawned on me that this was not the Covid cowboy lifestyle I had envisioned. John Wayne would never pillage another cowpoke's saddlebags or eat discarded fries from the Five Guys dumpster. Real cowboys didn't have to worry about someone coughing deadly droplets all over their bedroll or drunkenly pissing on their head when they were crammed together in a culvert.

I made my way north, ending up on the beaches near Santa Pulmo. With all the Corona restrictions, the area was nearly empty, and I was enjoying my own Gilligan's Island paradise, until a freak storm deluged the area. Seeking shelter, I noticed a beachfront mansion that looked abandoned. I crawled through a fence and found an open door to the pool house. There was a bar refrigerator well-stocked with Asahi beer and good Central Coast sauvignon blanc, which complimented the salty snacks I discovered in a drawer. I helped myself to a taste of Dreamy McPotsy I found in a drawer. I was in heaven, riding out the storm; I binge-watched *Girls* and *The Sopranos* on the huge flat screen (I'd never had HBO, and as they say, it's not TV), and when I didn't see lights in the main house, I even took the risk of firing up the hot tub.

That night, gale-force winds tore off the back screen to the mansion, and the door, which must have been ajar, blew open. In the reflection from the landscape lighting, I could see rain drenching the hardwood floors, and I decided to repay the hospitality by closing up the place. I crept through the doorway, and at first just listened, trying to discern indoor activity from the windy racket. Hearing nothing, I moved deeper into the building. A four-foot-wide puddle permeated the wide cherry planks, and I found dishtowels in the kitchen to sop up the mess. Cowboys never burglarize houses, and I had no intent of stealing, but there is a rule of the range that you offer travelers sustenance. While I was appreciative of the crunchy food I had enjoyed, my body was craving something that did not contain canola oil and acrylamide.

I wanted greens and was thrilled to discover the refrigerator was overflowing with vegetables and rare species of fruit only available to Range Rover and Tesla owners. It appeared there had been a party, the shelves stacked with bite-size cheese and cold cuts, and a huge kale salad. I found bagels and lox, which I slathered with designer mustard. I helped myself to a coconut cupcake from a round plastic container.

Satiated, I decided to explore the house. The living room alone was larger than any home I had ever occupied, decorated with sleek wooden furniture and impressionistic art. I assumed the owners had a flower fetish—or perhaps owned FTD—as there were dozens of arrangements scattered about the entry. A week or two past their expiration dates, they perfumed with fragrant decay. Upon closer examination, I realized they were funeral bouquets, with cards offering sympathy for "Riley." There was a small pile of obituary notices on the coffee table, and I stopped to read about a pretty woman named Riley's short life and quick death from Corona.

At the rear of the house, I discovered a ten-seat home theater and an arcade with a pool table, pinball machines, and video games. The walls were lined with photos, mostly of Riley, lips puffed to throw the camera a kiss. She struck me as the kind of person that really enjoyed having her photo taken. A few featured Riley and an older man, I assumed to be her husband, at black-tie events surrounded by politicians and C-level celebrities. I popped open another Asahi and stopped to shoot a game of eight-ball.

I was mounting the stairs to explore the second floor when I heard the moan, a death rattle that froze me in position. I was set to flee when the sound transformed into a soft plea. *Ahhhh*. I crept down the hallway and peered into a massive bedroom. In the dim light, I could see a shirtless man lying crossways on a big bed, one hand blindly fumbling on the nightstand.

"Do you need help?" I asked softly, worried that a heart attack caused by the appearance of a stranger in his bedroom might finish him off.

"Water," he said. "Burning up."

The glass and pitcher next to the bed were empty, but as I approached, he yelped, "Covid. Stay back." I rushed to the kitchen and filled a large container with ice water, pulled up the nylon gaiter I'd been wearing for the last three months, poured him a glass, and helped him bring it to his lips. His skin was slick. Sweat had pooled on the mattress, leaving a dark stain that outlined his body like a snow angel.

"Stay back," he coughed. Given my living circumstances over the last few months, I'd given a lot of thought to catching Corona, deciding I'd either already had it—some kind of flu had knocked the hell out of me in early March—or if not, it was probably inevitable I would catch it. While I wasn't looking forward to it, I figured a healthy twenty-five-year-old could weather the storm. However, this guy gave me pause. I'd never actually seen anyone seriously infected. He looked like an Auschwitz survivor, all bones and slick yellow flesh. Still, I'd eaten his pretzels, bagels, and kale and figured I owed him something.

"I'll call 911."

"No. The hospital would be worse. My wife died there. I want to stay here."

"Listen, you don't look good," I argued. "You need a doctor."

He motioned for more water, and I helped him raise the glass. "Just have to break the fever. Maybe I live, maybe I die. I don't care."

"Dude," I said. "That's the fever talking. Look at this house. If I owned it, I'd want to live forever. This place would make Jay-Z jealous."

"No doctor," he ordered.

"Okay," I said. "But we need to get you cleaned up. Get some food and fluids into you. You can't stay in that bed. It's soaked. If you have trouble breathing, I'm calling an ambulance, no matter what you say."

He insisted I mask him, then he wrapped an arm around my neck, and I helped him into the bathroom. There was a walk-in shower big enough to bathe a football team. I helped him strip off his sweatpants, set the water lukewarm, and propped him up while he rinsed off. I know it sounds odd, a man helping another man shower, but it felt familiar to me. When I was ten, my father spent eight months rusting away from cancer, forced to abandon all dignity as Mom and I washed, diapered, and spoon-fed him until a compassionate doctor overprescribed morphine.

I found a pair of boxers and led him across the hall into an equally impressive guest bedroom. He moaned in pleasure at the sensation of clean sheets and a fluffed pillow. "I'll get you something to eat," I said, and he croaked thanks. I heated a can of Paul Newman chicken noodle soup, buttered some bread, and poured a big glass of Gatorade. I wasn't sure if it was appropriate for Covid, but I gave him three Advil I found in the bathroom. He allowed me to feed him, murmured more gratitude, and before drifting off, said, "Don't catch this. It sucks."

I slept in a bedroom I found downstairs, rising several times during the night to make sure he was still breathing. At about four in the morning, I discovered he was awake and helped him drink more water. He seemed to be feeling better.

"Who are you?" he asked.

"Isaac."

"Hi, Isaac. I'm Randall. I appreciate your help, but I can't help but wonder how you came to be in my house?"

With nothing to lose, I explained how I had taken refuge in the cabana and entered the home. "I wasn't going to steal anything. I really did come in to keep the place from getting damaged, though I did help myself to a little food. But I didn't touch anything else."

Randall smiled. "I'm pretty sure if you meant any harm, you wouldn't be here now. Eat as much as you want. And if you see something you need, feel free to take it. I have plenty. Doesn't matter to me."

"I'm sorry about your wife." I had no idea what else to say.

He started to tear up. "Bad fucking year, isn't it?" He seemed to still be floating in a fever dream.

"You got that right."

"You know, Riley didn't love me," he said. "She was having affairs. Just with me for the money, I guess. I'm the stupid, silly older man that fell for her. Not sure if that makes her death better or worse."

"I don't believe that," I said. "You're a smart, good-looking, successful guy. I bet she was crazy about you. Sometimes people just make mistakes."

"I'm a fucking idiot," he said. "She's dead. She didn't care about me. And the problem is I really, really miss her, though for the life of me, I don't know why."

"Why are you here all alone? Is there someone I can call? Family or a friend? You need someone to take care of you."

"I don't want to be taken care of," he said.

"Sure you do," I said. "Who can I call?"

"There's nobody. Imagine getting to my age and not a soul in the world cares about you. My only family is a sister who hates me, and she lives back East. We moved to Santa Pulmo last year because Riley loved it. I worked all the time and didn't make any friends. I was hardly ever here. Maybe that's why she cheated."

"That's the fever talking," I said. "I bet a guy like you has hundreds of friends."

But he had nodded off to sleep.

For the next four days, I played nurse until Randall was well enough to move around on his own. In the afternoons, he recuperated by the pool, where I poured him glass after glass of lemon mineral water and fattened him up with plates of roasted chicken, lamb chops, and pasta. I'd spent years in food service before and during college, working as a fry cook and a sous chef. I even ran the kitchen at an Olive Garden, so I knew what I was doing. In fact, I'd considered going to cooking school before deciding there was a lot more money in computers.

I was surprised Randall would welcome a stranger into his home and allow him free reign, even handing me a credit card so I could arrange grocery delivery, but he seemed completely comfortable with our arrangement. At night, we'd retire to the movie theater to eat popcorn and sometimes watch John Wayne films. I shared my Covid cowboy philosophy, which made him laugh, but also revealed our joint love of the Duke.

I assumed that rich people only liked to talk about themselves, but Randall seemed very curious about me, and he had a therapist's touch, pulling out memories I thought I had permanently buried. One night, we traded mommy issues.

"My Dad died when I was ten. Leukemia," I told him. "He was a heavy drinker and smoker, which didn't help the situation, but he was a pretty good guy. Mom kind of died with him; it just took her longer. They were in love, and she never really recovered. We didn't have any money and had to move around a lot, from doublewide to doublewide. She'd take temp jobs, sometimes work as a dog groomer, and then we'd get a few months behind on rent, and we'd pack up in the middle of the night and move on. The day I graduated from high school, she was killed in a car wreck. She knew I loved this pizza—Don Leone's—and she drove across town to get one so we could celebrate. Drunk guy in an Escalade ran a light. I guess in some ways you could say it was my fault."

"Jesus," Randall said. "I'm sorry. There's no way it was your fault. Just a terrible luck of the draw. Do you have more family?"

"I've got an uncle somewhere. My dad's older brother, but I never knew him. Dad said he went to Canada to avoid Vietnam."

"So, you've been alone since you were seventeen?"

"I save a fortune on gifts on Mother and Father's Day."

Randall reached over to give my shoulder a squeeze. I instinctively recoiled the way men are conditioned to do when touched by another male, but sensing nothing nefarious, I let my shoulder relax into his hand, memories of my father flooding over me.

"What kind of pizza?" Randall asked.

"What do you mean?"

"What's your favorite pizza?"

"You'll laugh. You might even be offended."

"It's okay. This is a safe space."

"Hawaiian," I said. "Canadian bacon. Pineapple. Heavy on the red sauce."

"You're a sick kid."

The next day, he was almost back to normal, and I assumed it was time for me to leave. "Listen," I told him over an impressive Niçoise I had whipped up for lunch. I'd had fresh tuna and green beans delivered that morning. "I guess I'll be taking off this afternoon since you're doing well."

He looked up in surprise. "Where are you going?"

"Keep heading north. Find another mansion to break into," I laughed.

"You're welcome to stay here. It's rough out there right now."

"Thanks, but I don't want to overstay my welcome."

"Listen. How would you like a job?"

"Doing what?" I asked, surprised.

"Cook mainly. You're good at it. Plus, you're a techie guy. I can't get the music to work in the living room anymore, and the Crestron is always giving me an error message. I could use help around here, especially with no staff anymore."

"So, I'd be the chef? And the AV guy? Maybe the butler?"

"Yeah," he said. "Slop the pigs, chauffeur me around in the Rolls, steam my smoking jacket, tend the garden, scrub my back when I bathe. All the normal stuff."

"As far as I know, you don't have pigs or a Rolls Royce." I laughed. "I don't know if you remember, but I scrubbed your back the night we met, and I think that should be the only time we bathe together. But I would like to plant a garden."

"Great. Grow some tomatoes. It pays room and board and two grand a week."

"Jesus, really? Two thousand dollars a week?"

"What, not enough?"

"That's really generous of you, but I need to clarify…is there anything else you are expecting?"

Randall laughed. "Yes, you'd be required to wear a Speedo, a mesh T-shirt, and a ball gag on Saturday night. Maybe perform a few Epstein duties." He paused. "Isaac, I assure you this is a legitimate offer of employment."

I really wasn't accustomed to good things happening to me and was a little stunned by the offer. "Do I call you boss?"

"Boss, Jefe, Your Grace, Randall. They all work."

That night he ordered a Hawaiian pizza to celebrate my new position.

For the first time I really loved my work and looked forward to getting up every morning. I took enormous pride in the property, making sure everything was perfect. Randall insisted that we provide as many jobs in the community as possible, which was challenging during Covid, but I oversaw a cleanup of the grounds, had all the fences improved and repaired, retiled the pool, and planted a huge garden. I reprogrammed the household electronics and added new security. I cleaned, painted, polished, waterproofed, and disinfected.

I gave great thought and planning to the meals, still concerned with Randall's health after Covid. While he seemed fine physically, his depression was worsening. He was sleeping most of the time, and when he did move, he was listless and distracted; he was always kind to me, but he had the look of a man in pain. Granted, I had never known him during his healthiest days, but growing up with my folks, I learned a lot about mental health, and he was slipping.

For a person as accomplished as Randall, he seemed to have very little human interaction. His phone never rang unless there was a business issue. I'd catch him staring sadly at photos of himself and Riley. I realized that if he had died in that house weeks earlier, nobody except his office would be looking for him.

YOU CANNOT BE RAISED poor and believe the "money doesn't buy happiness" adage. Rich folks seem a lot happier than the people I know, and if money can't buy happiness, it does buy a lot of stuff that makes you happy. I was thrilled with my new luxe lifestyle, and initially, I was a bit disgusted by the fact that Randall didn't understand his privilege. But it became my goal to help him find joy, not only because he was my benefactor, but also because he seemed to be a man just looking for an outlet for his kindness.

I began documenting all the things that gave him pleasure: penne arrabbiata, Scorsese films, Carl Hiaasen novels, the creepy painting in the living room by some dude named Liu Wei, Stoli martinis, anything Jessica Chastain, *Seinfeld* re-runs, *Ms. Pac Man*.

There was no common thread.

Then one day at breakfast, he handed me an envelope. "A little bonus for all your good work," he said, beaming with the widest smile I had never seen on his face. Inside there was a notice from The

University of Phoenix confirming that my student debt of $63,480 was paid in full.

"What's this?" I said, stunned.

"Like I said, a little reward for the great job you're doing here. I didn't want you to be starting out in life with all that debt."

"This is more than a little reward, it's..." I really did not know what to say, and I'm embarrassed to admit it, but I started crying. I was trying to hide the tears by turning to the side to rub my eyes, as if I was having an allergy attack, instead of being dumbstruck by the greatest act of generosity I had ever experienced. When I looked up at Randall, I realized he was the only one in the room happier than me.

The next afternoon when the front gate buzzed with a delivery from Whole Foods, Randall asked how much I tipped the driver. "Twenty percent," I replied. "On the app."

"Let's do better," he said, and pulled three hundred dollars out of his wallet.

"You want to tip three hundred dollars for an eighty-dollar delivery?"

"Yep. Going forward, I'm going to keep an envelope with cash in the drawer here," he motioned at a cabinet. "Tip everyone at least a hundred bucks, double or triple that if you really like them."

"Are you sure?"

"It's only money, and people need it more than I do," he said, with the same gleeful look he had the previous day.

And there it was...the thing that gave Randall joy.

THE NEXT MORNING DURING breakfast, Randall pointed to a story he was reading in the *Santa Pulmo Explorer*. "It says the food bank is out of food. Did you ever go there?"

"Sure. When I first arrived, I got a sack of groceries. That's how I fed myself when I was living on the beach. I've been to dozens of food banks."

He asked a series of questions about how it all worked. "So, you waited in line for three hours for a bag of rice and some bread, tuna, and tomatoes," he said in amazement. "I didn't even know we had a food bank."

"Why would you?" I laughed.

"Yeah, why would I? I've come to realize I'm not as smart as I thought. I understand business, and the stock market, and a lot of other rich white man stuff, but I'm pretty much an idiot when it comes to how the real world operates."

"I don't know about that."

"It's true," Randall said. "Rich people fill their lives with useless knowledge and bizarre possessions."

"Like what?"

Randall chuckled. "Well, I'm one of five hundred people in the country that can actually tie a bow tie. I paid seven thousand dollars for a box that winds my watches. I have definite opinions on the most comfortable mid-range private jet. My toilet seat is heated, vibrates, and shoots warm water up my ass."

"I've used your toilet, and it is a thing of beauty," I said defensively. "I fondly call it the electric ass washing machine. Please don't make fun of it because it's my favorite thing in this wonderful house."

"Stay out of my bathroom." Randall smiled. "I brush my teeth with a three-hundred-dollar rechargeable toothbrush that connects to an app to tell me when I've brushed long enough, as if we need technology to determine when our mouth feels clean. I paid six thousand dollars for a white dinner jacket I've never worn because I hate going to events where you would be expected to wear a white dinner jacket. Before Covid, I used to pay a woman two hundred dollars to cut my hair—which didn't look any better than the job they would do at Supercuts—but I liked the neck rub she gave me afterward."

"For two hundred dollars you could get more than your neck rubbed."

Randall frowned and continued. "I can explain what a convertible asset swap is, but I have no idea how much a gallon of milk costs. I don't know how much minimum wage is, nor do I have any idea how much the average American makes. Last year, I paid eight thousand dollars for two tickets to see Bruce Springsteen on Broadway, even though I hate Bruce Springsteen. I shell out an extra hundred dollars to have little pieces of truffle the size of your fingernail shaved onto my pasta. Even though I hate truffles. Tastes like ass. There's a bottle of wine in the cellar worth ten thousand dollars. I could go on. It's fucking insane."

"Let's cure some of that insanity," I said. "Which bottle of wine is it? I'll go get it, and we will drink it right now so it doesn't torment you."

"I'm being serious."

"Boss, you're rich. You buy nice stuff. You don't need to worry about how much things cost. That doesn't make you a bad person. If I were rich, I'd put truffles on everything. Cereal, turkey sandwiches, everything. And I would dine sitting on my electric ass washing machine while Mila Kunis rubbed my neck and brushed my teeth."

"That's an awful visual. But my point is, maybe it's time for me to crawl out of the bubble."

"I don't know," I said, gesturing around. "It's a pretty nice bubble. Do you mind if I stay?"

He queried me about what it was like being homeless, and not the normal, "Wow, I bet it's scary" questions. People like to visualize homelessness as if it were some kind of *Escape from New York* adventure, all your time spent dodging predators. That's part of it, but the real challenge is overcoming the profound sense of degradation so you can concentrate on finding food that won't clog your arteries, a safe spot to sleep, and a reasonably clean place to take a shit.

Randall is quick and solution-focused—he reminds me of a Vulcan with a sense of humor—and he queried me on the logistics. How do shelters work? What about medical care and food sources?

He took copious notes the entire time as if he was interviewing me for the *New York Times.*

That evening, he showed me a series of articles he had printed out. "None of this makes sense," he said, gesturing at the first one. "Crops are rotting in the field fifty miles from here because we deported the people that pick them, or because the packaging plants are closed due to Covid. Even if the plants were open, it wouldn't help anyone here, because the system is designed to send food to a Costco in Chicago, or the Whole Foods in Detroit, and other places that require special packaging. Add to that, since the restaurants closed, the folks who know how to prepare food are out of jobs, while others go hungry. People are going broke and starving for no good reason."

"Hey, you'll go crazy if you try to find a logical reason for poverty. There's more than enough for everybody, but some people just don't like to share."

"Yeah. It's the trickle-down economics bullshit." he agreed. "If everyone gives their money to the rich, it will trickle down to the folks that need it. But rich people didn't get the memo. Guys like me pour their money into the stock market and buy white dinner jackets, a ten-thousand-dollar bottle of wine, and a fancy toothbrush."

Five days later, Randall announced we were taking a trip. I was surprised, as I'd never seen him leave the house, but he had a new energy that I loved. He had been cagey about where we were going. "Just a little joyride. Get some air." We headed an hour north and pulled off the freeway to traverse a series of dirt roads until he pulled over near a big farm. On our right a dozen workers were picking tomatoes, filling plastic crates pulled by a tractor. On the left, a crew harvested what appeared to be broccoli. The air was verdant and slightly fecal. Everyone was at least fifty feet apart.

"Does that look Covid safe to you?" he asked.

"Yeah, I would think so. Working outdoors, nobody close together. Looks about as safe as you could be."

"I don't want to get anyone sick."

"What did you do, go into the farming business?"

"In a manner of speaking," he said as we drove toward a cluster of buildings in the distance. "This is the Hawthorne Farm, one of those I read about that had crops ready to rot in the field. That didn't make sense to me, so I financed a harvest crew, and I'm paying Hawthorne a fair price for the vegetables, which keeps them in business. The packing plant is closed, so I've arranged for trucks to pick up the produce and distribute it to food banks up and down the coast." We pulled next to an enormous barn. A forklift was loading crates onto a semi. "You don't need packaging for the food banks, so it works out great."

"I thought the farm was having trouble getting workers."

"They were, but we came up with a solution. Many of the workers were still around but were afraid of being deported, so I'm paying them in cash. Plus, we were able to pick up quite a few people just out of work. There's twenty-five thousand in the bag in the backseat, which will cover us for the week. Everyone is tested before they can work. There's a nurse in the barn checking everybody out."

"How did you get the tests?" I asked. "I thought they were hard to come by."

"I know a guy who knows a guy," Randall smiled. "I think these tests were supposed to go to the NBA. I'm not much of a basketball fan." He pulled on his mask, grabbed the bag, and walked over to a big guy who looked like the foreman. As they talked, a food truck pulled into the clearing, and a man jumped out to open it up and set folding chairs and tables over a wide area.

When Randall climbed back into the car, he motioned at the truck. "The Soup & Sandwich Nazi. Best food truck in Santa Pulmo. They used to park near the courthouse. I'd go there once a week. Poor guy had to shut down when there was no lunch trade downtown, so I hired him to come out here and serve the workers. He was thrilled."

Randall explained more of the logistics as we drove back to Santa Pulmo. "When the trucks deliver to the food bank, they will also make a few other stops. I rented a couple kitchens from restaurants that are shut down," he said. "Hired back some of the staff, and I bought all the food that was just sitting in storage since they closed. They're going to start making takeout meals for the shelters and for unemployed folks who can't afford food. To help finance the operation, we're also selling meals for takeout and delivery. I hired some of the wait staff to handle that. This is the way trickle-down economics does work. Grow food, provide jobs, feed people."

As we neared Santa Pulmo, he pulled off the highway into an area that mainly catered to freeway travelers, with a truck stop, a service station, and two budget motels. He veered into the parking lot of the Super 8. "This place closed down a month ago. Not many people traveling during a pandemic. I got a good deal to rent it for a few months. We're going to offer temporary housing to the homeless starting in a few days. The nurse will check the workers out in the morning at the farm and then come here to test tenants before they can check in. We will try to keep it as Covid-free as possible. I've hired a couple more of the food trucks to park in the lot and provide meals."

"Jesus," I said. "You're a one-man Salvation Army. You're going to pay for all of this?"

"For the time being," Randall said. "I've committed five million dollars, and I'm going to start working the phones to get donations from people that owe me a favor. It's a big list. I think I can convince folks that during Covid, we don't need to buy watch winders or truffles. Feeding people might be a better investment."

"So, you're single-handedly going to end hunger and homelessness."

"Not by a long shot. I will make a little tiny dent in this area, and maybe it will inspire others. Maybe we can turn this into some kind of movement. And that brings me to your new job."

"New job?" I said defensively. "I'm really enjoying my current employment."

"You didn't go to college to clean my house. I probably wouldn't have taken on this project if I hadn't met you, so you have a big role. We're missing some crucial technology that makes this thing work. I don't want people to wait in line for hours at a food bank or come all the way out here just to discover the place is full. I want you to write a simple app that lets people know when food will be arriving and set up an appointment for pick up so nobody wastes time or risks Covid in a crowd. They should also be able to check on housing availability and schedule an appointment for a test. All of that can integrate into the delivery schedule so we can keep the food banks apprised of delivery times and exactly what's going to be delivered."

"That's a big piece of technology. While I did graduate Maga Cum Suckie from the renowned University of Phoenix, it might exceed my skill level a bit."

"I assume maybe some of your coworkers are now unemployed, since Penney's has gone the way of Blockbuster and Kmart?" Randall asked.

"Probably."

"Hire a few of the best and fast-track the project."

I considered the fact that the most talented coder I knew was my old boss—the man who refused to give me a reference—but there were no hard feelings. He probably needed a job, and I looked forward to giving him a call.

"Randall," I joked. "You apparently did not get the rich guy memo. You're supposed to be investing your money in space exploration and personal monuments. Maybe have a replica of your face chiseled into some mountain or buy a big building to name after yourself."

"Let's tackle that after nobody is starving," he said.

By Christmas, we had six farms supplying sixty food banks and twenty-four restaurants converted to free kitchens up and down the coast: a couple hundred of the formerly unemployed feeding thousands of people. NPR profiled the endeavor on *Morning Edition*, and between PR and Randall's outreach, donations were pouring in. Several of the major food companies were now contributing to the cause.

The app was not without its bugs, but it worked reasonably well and was getting better every day. As expected, my old boss was much more adept at the technology than I was, and he had taken over management.

I assumed a role for which I was better suited, spending a lot of time on the road showing people how to use the app. I would do interviews with local press to publicize the program and travel to new food banks and kitchens to help them set up the ordering and tracking capability. I would venture into homeless camps—a place I did not miss but knew all too well—to show them how to use the service. I know it seems odd, but most of the homeless are connected, and I would get them to download the app and encourage them to spread the details on food and lodging to those who didn't have a phone. I would carry cases of masks to distribute.

Randall would often come with me, especially when we were setting up new food distribution. He was a new man with refreshed purpose and energy, and he loved seeing the program expand. Sometimes, when we were speeding down the road, I realized we were living my dream, too.

My favorite Westerns feature the reluctant hero. Alan Ladd as Shane, defending the town from outlaws. John Wayne secretly saving Jimmy Stewart in *The Man Who Shot Liberty Valance*. *The Magnificent Seven* riding in to protect the village. They were the greatest cowboys.

Now, here comes Randall and me, riding the range, rolling into a new town to make life just a little bit better for those in need. Protect the innocent. Just like the Duke. Covid Cowboys.

Verse VI

THE LIE

WHENEVER SHE PERUSED OLD family photo albums, Sydney longed for the man her uncle used to be. Leonard Feldman had served with distinction in Vietnam and returned to pursue a degree in business from Santa Pulmo State—courtesy of the GI Bill—followed by a long career in hardware. He'd spent ten years working as regional manager for True Value before opening his own store in 1986. Feldman's quickly became a Santa Pulmo institution, the locals happy to favor a homegrown business over the mega-stores in Paso Grande. In turn, Len embraced the community, supporting local fund drives, sponsoring baseball teams, always happy to make space available to sell Girl Scout cookies and Kiwanis apples. He was the jovial fix-it guy, greeting customers like close friends, often personally delivering orders. On more than one occasion, he would answer a nighttime call from a panicked customer suffering a burst pipe or a leaking water heater, unable to find a plumber. Uncle Len, sometimes still wearing his pajama top, would trudge over to their house with his tool kit, usually making the repair gratis.

Sydney would stop to visit him on her way home from school, pulling her bike into the loading dock, traversing heavy aisles in search of her uncle. She'd discover him stacking light bulbs or wrenches, festooned in a red vest with a nametag that proclaimed *LEONARD—HEAD BOTTLEWASHER*. When she shouted, "Hey, Uncle Len," he'd drop his reading glasses, blink happily as if he hadn't seen her in years, and say something corny like, "Hey, what's Julia Roberts doing here?"

The store was famous for the free popcorn handed out to shoppers; the aroma of melted butter mixed with the tang of gear oil wafting through aisles. Uncle Len would lead her to the big red machine near the front door, grab two sacks, and direct her to the employee break room, popping two Cokes out of the machine. Her uncle ascribed to the retail theory that people buy more when listening to Frank Sinatra, so all day long, he played a loop of the Chairman's greatest hits, substituting Christmas albums during the holiday season. Sometimes, he would grab Sydney and twirl her, mouthing the words to "I've Got You Under My Skin" or "Fly Me to the Moon" as she giggled and tried to follow his awkward steps.

Sydney was accustomed to her parents' perfunctory "How was your day?" delivered as she rushed through the house. However, when Uncle Len asked the question, he seemed genuinely interested. She would relate often painful tales of math tests, mean girls, and her newest crush, as he nodded excitedly, occasionally rubbing his buzz cut as if sharpening his hand.

In 1992, on her fourteenth birthday, he threw her a surprise party. A dozen friends were waiting on the beach in front of his house as Uncle Len, clad in his faded Hawaiian shirt and a silly chef's hat, circulated among them with a tray of hot dogs and hamburgers. Though he was strictly an easy listening and country music fan, he'd gone to the trouble of purchasing a few albums he thought Sydney and her friends might enjoy, with Michael Jackson and Right Said Fred blasting out speakers dragged to the deck.

At sunset, he rolled a wheelbarrow from the garage loaded with bamboo Tiki torches, shoving them in the sand in an oval. He pulled Sydney to the center for an embarrassing performance to "I'm Too Sexy," Uncle Len doing his best Chris Farley impression, and as Sydney and her friends continued to dance, he brought out a tray of champagne glasses, filled them with non-alcoholic sparkling wine, and led a birthday toast to his niece.

After everyone went home, he presented her with a small package, professionally wrapped with a Kane Brothers sticker. Sydney had never received a gift that came from a real jewelry store and was wide-eyed as he handed it to her.

"Fancy," she said, smiling.

"Better get used to nice presents. You're a beautiful young woman now. Soon men will be lining up with gifts trying to impress you."

She gasped when she opened that green leather case and pulled out the Bulova watch. Gold with a white face, it was feminine and dainty and wonderfully grown-up. Her initials were engraved in tiny letters on the back.

"Sorry, but you can't return it," he laughed as she read the inscription.

"I would never do that," she said, throwing her arms around his neck. "I love it. Thank you so much."

"Sydney," he said, turning serious. "You know, you can always count on me. No matter what. I'll always be there for you. Happy Birthday."

At that moment, she thought her Uncle Len was the greatest man in the world.

SOMETIMES, SYDNEY WOULD TRY to pinpoint the date when her uncle morphed into someone angry and unrecognizable. She had a faint memory of stopping by the store during her junior year of high school and discovering him in his office, Rush Limbaugh's radio show blaring.

"You should listen to this guy," he said excitedly. "He makes a lot of sense."

Curious, Sydney tuned in over the next couple of days, and decided that Uncle Len was joking. From what she could tell, the radio personality was just another shock jock spewing whatever pabulum necessary to draw attention. She sometimes listened to

Howard Stern's program, which she found juvenile—one long fart joke—but amusing. Though Rush's tantrums seemed more mean-spirited, she assumed Uncle Len found something entertaining about his non-stop litany of social grievances.

However, it soon became clear that her uncle's love of Limbaugh was emblematic of a much more profound change in attitude. Bill Clinton filled him with a festering hate. Uncle Len had always been a Republican, serving on Reagan's and Bush Senior's local campaign committees. She'd considered her uncle the classic compassionate conservative, in love with the idea of American exceptionalism, Ford not Toyota, strong defense, low taxes, and a devotion to "in God we trust," even though she'd never seen him attend church and suspected he might be an atheist.

Uncle Len would pontificate about the superiority of American-made tools, but it was charmingly patriotic. America was the Rotary Club, cheap gasoline, and stoic white men running the show. Clinton represented something dangerous: a sexy southern redneck that had attended Oxford and played the saxophone on Johnny Carson. The Elvis of politicians. His mouthy wife was pushy and harsh, unwilling to adhere to housewife norms conservative men found acceptable.

Even though Uncle Len's first marriage had ended due to his own infidelity, he was outraged by the president's affairs, which for some reason focused him on Hillary. "She's just as guilty as he is. Stays with him when he abuses all those young girls. I'm sure she's a lesbo anyway and doesn't care. The two just want to make money, and they'll do anything to stay in power." When the president remained popular and successful, it fueled even wilder theories. "The man is a serial killer. Had at least thirty people murdered." Normally sedate Sunday family dinners were now devoted to gripes, conspiracy theories, and sexism that Sydney increasingly found offensive.

That was also when Sydney noticed her uncle's creeping racism. He'd spout ridiculous stories about a secret Jewish cabal that sounded more like a plot line in a Jack Higgens novel. The hardware store enjoyed robust trade from the many Hispanic workers that kept Santa Pulmo and the surrounding area operating, and on many occasions, Sydney had witnessed Uncle Len greet Mexican customers like old friends, shouting friendly welcomes in bad Spanglish. Now, the conservative commentators he favored had convinced him his former friends and customers were an invading force.

"Your uncle's a dick, or maybe he's going senile," her friend Maria Alvarez told her one afternoon. "My dad told me he follows him around the store like he's a shoplifter, and he heard him call my cousin Danny a 'dirty fucking Pedro.'"

Sydney had reached an age when she felt comfortable debating with her uncle during family gatherings, especially when it came to his racist and sexist ideas. "Uncle Len, you've told me stories about Vietnam," she said. "About how great the Hispanic and black soldiers were. You said you'd rather have them backing you up than the white guys."

Len nodded. "That's true. They make good soldiers. However, that doesn't mean we need to let them take over the country. At its core, America is white and Christian. That's what's made us the greatest nation in the world. We can't forget that."

"Uncle Len, at its core, this country is Native American, except for the fact that the white invaders killed most of them, which wasn't very Christian," Sydney countered. "And this area had a Hispanic population long before white people came here. Maria Alvarez's family moved to this valley in the 1870s. Our family didn't immigrate to America until 1910."

"Quit being silly," Uncle Len poo-pooed. "You should just be happy you were born white."

A MAJOR FISSURE IN Sydney's relationship with her uncle occurred during her senior year of high school. Sydney couldn't wait to tell

Uncle Len about the scholarship offer from UC Berkeley and was shocked by his reaction.

"Berkeley? You cannot go to that goddamn commie school. All they'll teach you there is how to do drugs and burn the flag." When Sydney stood her ground and informed him it was her school of choice, their relationship was forever altered.

She'd see him when she returned on holidays, careful to keep her temper in check from the onslaught of snide remarks. "How's it going up there in Commieville? Bet that campus smells pretty bad with all those filthy hippies."

"Uncle Len," she couldn't help replying, "you need to crawl out of the 1960s. The hippies disappeared thirty years ago. Now, they are running banks and Fortune 500 companies. They probably loan you money."

Sydney's parents, both bookish liberals, chose to ignore Uncle Len's werewolf-like transition. Her father, five years his junior, saw the good in everyone and chalked up his brother's anger to age, loneliness, and business anxiety. "Poor guy is getting older, just went through his second divorce—and by the way, he's going to have to sell the beach houses—plus he's losing customers to all the box stores. Cut him a break. He has a good heart. I know his politics seem nutty, but in the end, he will always do the right thing. Plus, he adores you like his own daughter."

However, the year she graduated from college, Sydney failed to feel any love from her uncle. She'd been cagey about her sexual preferences, finally finding the courage to bring her girlfriend home to meet the family. Her parents, as expected, cheerfully accepted the news, her mother confiding they had always suspected her sexual preference. However, when she introduced Dina to Uncle Len, her arm protectively wrapped around Dina's waist, as he flushed crimson, angrily announcing, "Disgusting," and stormed out of the house.

And that was the end of their relationship. When Sydney visited Santa Pulmo, her uncle was conspicuously absent. Her father weakly defended his brother, but in private, her mom would detail Len's descent. 9/11 had intensified his racism. He'd been taken to court in a high-profile lawsuit when he kicked a woman wearing a hijab out of the store. He had erected a billboard on the corner of his lot that spouted ultra-conservative talking points—the latest in homage to the NRA, which offended a good percentage of locals. "He used to be respected in Santa Pulmo," her mother said sadly. "People liked him and wanted to be around him. Now he's just the crazy, gun-loving racist that runs the hardware store."

The night Obama was elected, Sidney was attending a celebration at the St. Francis Hotel in San Francisco. After graduating from law school, she'd joined her dream firm in the city, and she and her coworkers were filled with euphoria and vodka tonics as they toasted America's youthful new leader. She knew her mother had supported Obama, and, wishing they could be together at the celebration, stepped into a hallway to call her.

"Hold on," her mother whispered into the phone, "I have to go outside. Len is here. He's drunk and spouting off. I've never seen him like this. He's saying such terrible things. I can't take it."

"Throw him out. There's no reason to put up with that."

"You know your father would never do that," she said. "He loves him no matter what. But Len is getting crazier. He was bragging he's been buying more guns—stocking up for the war—is how he puts it. He offered to bring your dad an AK47. Imagine that! I'm concerned he's going to accidentally shoot himself, or worse, someone else. He has also been hoarding gold, which he certainly cannot afford. One of those damn crazy commentators he likes is selling safes loaded with gold coins, and Len is spending everything he has on the crap. It's sad."

Sydney didn't invite Uncle Len to the wedding when she and Dina married a year later, but that didn't stop him from expressing his opinion. When she returned from their honeymoon, there was a card waiting. She was hoping for some kind of reconciliation as she opened it.

Sydney, my heart is broken by your perversion. You are breaking God's law and condemning yourself to an eternity in hell.

She threw the card away, determined never to speak to him again.

~

LEN DELIVERED THE FINAL blow to his own business when he posted *OBAMA IS A MUSLIM* on his billboard and replaced the happy Sinatra music with monitors mounted throughout Feldman's blaring Fox News.

"Len, people just want to go to the store and shop in peace," his brother tried to reason to him. "They don't care about your politics."

"America needs to know the truth. I'm performing a public service."

The residents of Santa Pulmo did not agree, and traffic to Feldman's came to a standstill. In 2016, Len was forced to sell the building to an apartment developer to pay off his debts and open a very scaled-down Feldman's. Sydney's mom drove her by the new store when she came home for Thanksgiving.

"Oh my God," Sidney said as they passed the store. "That's it?" The original Feldman's employed forty people in a shiny steel structure on a half city block, with a parking lot big enough to accommodate fifty cars. The new location, a small, stained block building that had been vacant since a video store shut down eight years earlier, was wedged between a motel that advertised "room rental by the hour" and a tattoo parlor. Feldman's was now manned by Len and one other full-time employee—an elderly gent who shared Len's political paranoia.

Sydney couldn't help but feel sympathy for her uncle. "Mom, this is so sad. I do not understand what happened to him. He was a big success, but now he's pathetic. He's destroyed everything."

"It's some kind of mental illness," her mother agreed. "He watches TV all day, or listens to those hateful radio shows, and believes all these awful things that aren't real. Somehow, he manifests the worst for himself."

While Trump's election added temporary validation to Len's beliefs, in liberal Santa Pulmo, it did not translate into improvement for his business, which just fueled his anger. On weekends, he would don his Trump red, white, and blue uniform, mount huge MAKE AMERICA GREAT AGAIN flags to his F150, and travel hundreds of miles to join caravans of other believers, often sleeping in the back of his truck.

To Sydney's alarm, after retiring from his accounting practice, her father began working at Feldman's part-time when the only other employee moved to Florida. "He's barely making it and can't afford any full-time help," he explained. "I need to give him a hand."

"Dad, he's toxic. He will just bring you down. You should enjoy your retirement."

Her mother had also had her fill of Uncle Len. His support of men accused of sexually abusing women was the last straw for her, and she refused to host the weekly dinners that had been a family tradition for decades. "The poor guy doesn't have anyone," her father pleaded. "Since I can't have him over to the house anymore, it's the only opportunity I have to see him. Three afternoons a week for a few hours. Just so he can run some errands. Plus, it gives me something to do."

When Covid hit, Sydney grew more concerned, especially when she learned Feldman's was deemed "essential" and would remain open. She phoned her folks, pleading with her dad to stay home. "Listen, this thing is serious," she said. "People are dying, especially old people. For God's sake, you've had cancer, and Mom has a heart condition. You're both in the high-risk category."

"Who are you calling old?" he joked. "I'm in the prime of my life."

"Dad, promise me you will stay home and stay away from the store. You and Mom need to quarantine and avoid Uncle Len."

"Okay, okay," he said.

Sydney subscribed to the online edition of the *Santa Pulmo Explorer* and perused the paper during her morning coffee. When

Covid swept through Moonlight Cove, she called her folks. "Mom, did you see that Liz Stickler and Rick Hughes died of Covid? I can't believe it."

"I know," she said. "The hospital is already full."

"I hope you two are staying safe. Dad's not going into the store, is he?"

"No, honey, we're quarantining. Don't worry. You just take care of yourself."

~

Sydney and Dina quickly adapted to the new Corona reality, negotiating every morning for precious broadband, while greatly improving their cooking skills and expanding their Netflix list. Sydney had taught her folks the wonders of Zoom, and every Sunday night, they had an online family cocktail hour, which unfortunately was often devoted to discussions about how rapidly society was deteriorating.

One morning, she clicked on the *Santa Pulmo Explorer*, only to be greeted by a defiant photo of her Uncle Len, standing in front of his store, with the headline, FELDMAN'S HARDWARE OWNER CITED FOR COVID VIOLATIONS. The story detailed how Len refused to wear a mask and didn't require patrons to be masked. "This entire Covid thing is a hoax," he told the reporter. "There's no way I am going to give up my civil liberties or make my customers give up theirs. They can put me in jail." There was no call to incarcerate Len, but the state did levy a thousand-dollar fine, with the threat to close him down if he didn't comply within a week. Len replied he would ignore the order, adding, "And there is no way in hell I am paying a government that is trying to strip me of my rights."

Sydney missed a call from her mother two days later and panicked when she listened to the voicemail. "Sydney, your dad and I are not feeling well. Heading into the doctor, and I will update you after we get checked out."

She was still shocked at how fast their Covid progressed. Her mother called her that afternoon to report they had both tested positive. Sydney performed her own tracing and pieced together the puzzle. Despite the fact her father had promised to stay away from his brother, she learned he had been going into the store to help. Len contracted the disease—in his case, it was mild and didn't require hospitalization—but she suspected he had infected Sydney's father, who in turn exposed her mother. They were not as fortunate as Len.

Sydney was helpless watching her parent's demise on her iPad. Her first impulse was to jump in her car and drive to Santa Pulmo, but the doctor advised against it. "We don't want you in the hospital. You wouldn't be able to get near them, and it just makes it more difficult for us. Since you can't be in a room with them, it's just easiest if you communicate online and not put yourself at risk."

It was a morbid way to lose her family, watching the life leak out of them as a nurse filmed from above, like some kind of snuff film. Sydney's father passed away five days later. Her mother lingered for three more weeks, the disease attacking her system from multiple angles, until she died of heart complications.

The following summer, she and Dina returned to Santa Pulmo to lead a small memorial on the beach, spreading her parents' ashes into the breeze, watching them dissipate across the bay. She had not invited Uncle Len and was relieved when he didn't make a surprise appearance. She'd envisioned—even craved—an angry showdown with him, but today was not a day for such pained emotions.

Sydney had planned to sell the house while she was home, but as she and Dina drove through town, they could sense the community breathing again. Most of the shops had reopened, and it felt odd and exhilarating to see people smiling, free of the masks that had hidden their emotions for over a year.

"How would you feel about moving here?" she asked Dina.

"Are you serious?"

"We've proven we can work remote. I wouldn't even mind opening a practice here. It could be good for you. There's going to be a demand for chefs again. It just feels right. Being in a community. There are some good people here. Long walks on the beach. Fresh sushi. We could never afford a house in the city. Wouldn't it be wonderful to have a home without a mortgage? What more could we want?"

Dina nodded. "I've always loved your folk's place. I think it would be incredible. But would that be okay for you? Can you deal with the bad memories?"

"Uncle Len is my only bad memory in Santa Pulmo," Sydney said. "Otherwise, I love it here."

"All right, let's do it," Dina said. "But just one thing, I need to take surfing lessons," she joked.

~

THE NEXT DAY, SYDNEY drove around town by herself, anxious to revisit old haunts, see all the changes that had taken place, and view Santa Pulmo once again through the eyes of a resident. She was thrilled to discover that Lazy Owl Coffee, which had reopened a couple times as different businesses under Covid, was once again a coffee and scone shop, and she stopped to buy her traditional vanilla latte. She felt a deep ache navigating the town without her parents. Driving by the grade school, she stopped at the corner where her mother would drop her off on rainy mornings. Her mom would reach over to button her jacket and always announce, "Go in there and be the smartest girl in the class," before delivering a kiss to her forehead.

The building that housed her father's old accounting firm was now a real estate office, and a woman was scrubbing the front window. Sydney remembered accompanying her dad to the office on Saturdays while he picked up paperwork, then heading to lunch at Burger Mania on the corner, where she always ordered the chili fries. Often, they would walk across the street to see a matinee at the Orpheum, her father even agreeing to sit through *Home Alone* twice.

She thought how wonderful it would be if her parents were alive. They would love watching Santa Pulmo emerge from its Covid cocoon, and she longed to hear them greet all their old friends, happy survivors who had made it through the war. They would be thrilled at the idea of her moving back. She and Dina had been considering having a baby, and it tore her apart to know her parents would never know their grandchild.

Operating on autopilot, she drove to the industrial section of town and found herself in front of Feldman's. Uncle Len's truck was parked at the rear of the building. She'd fanaticized about what she'd say to her uncle and figured if she were moving back, a confrontation was inevitable. Might as well get it over with, she reasoned, feeling her sadness recast as anger.

The store was open, but looked abandoned. It was dark and reeking of oily mold. Bars covering narrow windows cast shadows onto the floor, giving it the aura of a prison. The popcorn machine had been relocated to the new building but sat abandoned near the front counter. This place certainly didn't get enough traffic to justify using it, and from the yellow stains on the glass, she assumed it hadn't been cleaned in years. She could hear a television blaring from the office at the rear of the building. Her uncle, seated at his desk, *Fox and Friends* playing on an ancient Magnavox, didn't notice her. The cheerful television hosts were discussing whether a prominent Democratic senator might be an Iranian spy.

She blanched when she saw the pictures above his desk. There was a family portrait from her high school graduation, Uncle Len and her parents surrounding her with love. Next to that was a photo of Uncle Len and her dad taken when Len had returned from Vietnam, both young men looking fresh and vibrant, about to enter the prime of their lives. And the largest photo disturbed her the most…a shot of Sydney and Uncle Len dancing at her fourteenth birthday party.

He was swinging her under his arm, both laughing uncontrollably, as her friends clapped in the background.

Fox and Friends had moved on to a new subject, a large Chyron asking: IS KAMALA REALLY AMERICAN?

"Jesus, even after all that has happened, you still watch that crap."

He flinched in surprise. She was shocked at how old he looked, just a wizened old man. "Sydney..." he said in a fragile voice.

She unclasped the Bulova watch she had been wearing for almost thirty years and threw it at him. It struck him in the forehead, tearing old skin, and he dabbed at a spot of blood. "You lied," she screamed.

He looked at her in confusion. "What?"

"When you gave me that watch, you said you would always be there for me. I could depend on you. You loved me. It was all a lie." Uncle Len shrunk back into his seat. "And here you sit, still listening to this garbage," she said, gesturing at the television. "Like an addict that needs a fix."

The old man looked shocked and bent down to pick up the watch. "Sydney, please..." He held it up to her. "Of course, I love you."

"No," she said, and slapped it out of his hand. "I don't want it, and I want nothing to do with you. Look at all you lost," she pointed at the pictures again. "You had a family that adored you. A great business. You had friends, and people respected you. Now you have nothing. You threw it all away for them." She pointed at the television. "Your fake friends. They fed you lies to get you angry, so you'd buy guns and MAGA signs and gold and all the shit they peddle. They used you. And you allowed it, infecting everyone you know with their lies, until you finally killed my parents."

"Sydney, don't say that," he said, choking back tears. "I would never...I thought I was doing the right thing. I thought it was the truth."

"It wasn't. You chose hate over love and killed Mom and Dad," she said, turning to rush out of the shop. She was near the front of the store when she noticed a display on an endcap. PARTY ON THE

BEACH, the sign advertised. The rack held bamboo Tiki torches, canisters of citronella-scented fuel, and long lighters. She flashed back to her birthday, which enraged her even more. Grabbing a bottle of fuel, she poured it all over the display. She opened another and splashed it on the floor and adjoining shelves. She emptied a third onto the nearby racks that held paint and thinners. Ripping one of the lighters out of a package, she torched a rivulet running down the aisle, mesmerized as the flame raced around, lighting the shelves hot blue.

"What are you doing?" she heard Uncle Len yell. He was standing at the end of the aisle, looking even more shrunken and weak. "No!"

There was a whoosh, followed by a burst of heat as the Tiki display went up in six-foot flames. A rack of cloth bags behind the display was on fire, and burning liquid was spreading through the store.

"Get out," she said, pushing her uncle toward the front door, then giving him a final heave into the street. He stumbled, and tried to rush back in, but she shoved him again hard. He fell back, arms and legs splayed, wincing at the muffled explosions, as fire reached combustible cans.

Sydney walked to her car and turned. Uncle Len was rising painfully to his knees, covering his face with an elbow as a window blew out of the side of the building. He turned to face her in confusion, mouth agape, glassy eyes pleading, as he thrust an arm forward, her watch dangling from his right hand.

Verse VII

VIVA LAS VEGAS

LAUNCHED TO GREAT FANFARE in 2016, Viva Las Vegas was the third-largest cruise ship in the world. With twenty-five hundred staterooms and a capacity of five thousand passengers, it was big enough to house the entire town of Bisbee, Arizona.

The Viva was home to every possible recreational activity and luxury. In addition to multiple casinos, the big boat featured a ten-story waterslide; a bowling alley; a nine-hole virtual-screen golf course; a surfing beach powered by a million-dollar wave machine; Carrot Top's Comedy Club, which doubled as an afternoon bingo parlor; a nightly performance of *Hamilton*; and the popular Elvis Presley Theater, which each evening projected a disturbingly realistic hologram starring the long-dead superstar. The colossal spa offered twelve different styles of massage, including the "Ultimate Cleanse," which combined a painful Rolfing regiment with a pomegranate juice high colonic.

There were three Wolfgang Puck restaurants, the Blue Suede Shoes Lounge, and a Five Guys Burger that was open twenty-four hours a day. Clooney's served twenty-five variations of Nespresso and jumbo shots of Casamigos. The shopping mall housed twenty stores, including Gucci, Hugo Boss, James Pearse, and Viva Swim & Yoga Wear, which stocked an impressive selection of racy lingerie and sex toys, since there is something erotic about traveling in a tight-quartered floating city.

Environmentalists detested the vessel, calling it a mobile garbage dump. They cited the fact that the Viva emitted 450,000 gallons of sewage per week, while racking up multiple fines for dumping hazardous sludge across pristine coral reefs. The tiny Polynesian island of Hanalepo sued the cruise line, charging they had converted paradise into a cesspool. The Viva burned a particularly nasty low-grade fuel, producing the same amount of pollution per minute as seven hundred cars, the passengers blissfully unaware that while playingpickleball, they consumed the equivalent particulate matter of doing wind sprints in industrial Mumbai.

There was great dissension in the community when the Viva applied to dock near Santa Pulmo while on its Wonders of the Pacific Coast schedule. Many businesses were thrilled at the idea of thousands of tourists flooding the streets, but die-hard Santa Pulmoians protested, arguing that an influx of inebriated, poorly-dressed elderly people buying Chinese knickknacks emblazoned "Santa Pulmo" would destroy the town's charm, while polluting the pristine bay. Ultimately the city council denied the request, resulting in a vandal spray painting LIBTARDS HATE MONEY across the side of the courthouse.

The Viva faced a much more serious issue when passengers started dropping from Corona. The first cases were confirmed a few days after departing Manzanita, and within a week, the ship reported hundreds of sick passengers, with seventeen deaths and counting. Every port in Mexico and the United States refused Viva's request to disembark the sick cruisers. So while the US Government attempted to find a home for the Bahamian-registered ship owned by a Florida-based corporation with Irish tax status, it moored a quarter mile off Santa Pulmo's sandy beach, a ship of lepers. Daily, the captain of the Viva called the mayor of Santa Pulmo, begging to let them dock; his request was consistently denied.

Mayor Wheeler had his own Corona problems and did not intend to flood his streets with diseased tourists. The Covid disaster at Moonlight Cove permeated the town, and infected workers unwittingly spread the disease through the entire valley. The evolving outbreak at the county jail looked ominous. Santa Pulmo's small hospital was overrun, with zero capacity for outsiders.

The Viva was frequently home to onboard conventions, and on this sailing, the Mississippi-based Americans for Morality, a conservative organization primarily focused on an anti-gay, anti-Muslim, anti-women-wearing-pants agenda, was hosting two hundred supporters for their yearly meeting. In addition to daily workshops led by the leader of the organization, Reverend Tobias Wildmon, there were additional right-wing dignitaries onboard to deliver speeches, including Fox News commentator and former Miss Ohio, Kaylee Johansson; television icon Scott Baio; Pentecostal minister Elijah Wolf; and the mysterious publisher of TRUAMERICANPATRIOT.com, who simply went by the name General Patton.

Americans for Morality created tension among other passengers when posters promoting the day's lectures were displayed in the hallways. The captain received multiple complaints about advertisements for the *Hitler Was Muslim* and *God's Plan for the Obedient Wife* presentations. Tensions were further flamed when two venomous snakes Reverend Wolf was using for a church service escaped into the ventilation system.

When Covid hit the Viva, members of Americans for Morality, who most afternoons were ensconced on the Donny Osmond deck, glued to Fox, were skeptical of the seriousness of the situation.

"It's just the flu," Reverend Wildmon assured the flock. "But the press wants to use it to take the president down. More fake news. And besides, we're protected by Jesus." When Wildmon was one of the first to die, followed by seventeen other members who fell ill, the mood began to change. Suddenly, the Viva morphed from a fun ship into a floating prison.

Guests were restricted to their staterooms, except during staggered periods in which they were allowed to walk the decks, properly distanced, for a little exercise. The showrooms, casinos, and restaurants were closed—and instead, surly masked stewards delivered junior high cafeteria-quality food. Unbeknownst to anyone except a few crewmembers, one of the walk-in refrigerators was transformed into a morgue, with bodies double stacked next to industrial-sized canisters of Miracle Whip.

To make matters worse, extreme demand overloaded air conditioning and sanitary systems. Rooms topped one hundred degrees, while toilets overflowed with diseased sludge. Passengers were gasping for air on balconies, partially due to Covid, but also the result of putrid air circulating within their space.

Kaylee Johansson, Scott Baio, and General Patton had managed to slip into a closed lounge during their recreation period—celebrities afforded certain privileges—and were drinking canned margaritas when General Patton spoke up. "We have to get off this fucking death star; otherwise, we will perish at sea with these senior citizens." He tossed his empty can at a snake slithering along the wall.

"Do you think it's that serious?" Kaylee asked.

General Patton noticed that Kaylee had been honed by Fox to only react to sensationalistic headlines, so he tried to speak in a language she might comprehend. "I think that if we stay on this ship, we will die a horrible death where our lungs explode and blood streams out every orifice. In a few days, they'll be dumping dead bodies overboard like *The Sopranos*."

Kaylee blanched and began to cry. Baio pledged to call his friend the president, but everyone doubted that would work. "We're docked near Santa Pulmo," General Patton said. "I might have a solution."

~

DANNO WAS HAVING A bad month. Since he was outed as "patient zero" in the Moonlight Cove Covid outbreak, the press and angry families of the deceased residents of the retirement home had hounded him. There were daily death threats, and not only from livid survivors. Every day, he received an email from General Patton:

INTEREST ON YOUR DEBT IS ACCRUING AT $200 PER DAY, AND MY MOSSAD AGENTS WILL SOON BE VISITING.

The only good news was that Pugs had allowed him to bunk on his couch, and they had both been lucky enough to land part-time jobs delivering pot for Speedy Weedy. So, at least he had a little cash coming in, and unlike others quarantined, he was an essential employee, which allowed him to roam the empty streets.

Pugs tried to raise his spirits, holding a nightly cocktail hour, featuring homemade vodka and joints he managed to pilfer from daily deliveries. But Danno continued to vacillate between depression and fear, constantly looking out the window, searching for reporters or tough-looking bald men coming to collect.

One afternoon when Pugs walked into the apartment, Danno greeted him with a happy yell. "He's here, he's here," he said to his friend.

"Who?"

"General Patton. He's stuck on the ship out in the harbor. Look at this email."

I'M GOING TO GIVE YOU AN OPPORTUNITY TO SETTLE YOUR DEBT. MY ASSOCIATES AND I, ALL MAJOR CELEBRITIES, ARE BEING HELD AGAINST OUR WILL ON THE VIVA LAS VEGAS NEAR SANTA PULMO. I WANT YOU TO FIND A BOAT THAT WILL ACCOMMODATE FOUR PASSENGERS AND PICK US UP TOMORROW AT MIDNIGHT. DO THAT AND I WILL FORGIVE THE DEBT. GENERAL PATTON.

"Wow," Pugs said. "That's weird. Why wouldn't he just have his Mossad guys come get him? They probably have some kind of super cool speedboat."

"Who cares why?" Danno said. "This is a big break. Doesn't your cousin have a boat?"

"Well, technically it's a raft. But it has a motor and floats."

"Perfect," Danno said, already emailing General Patton.

Before he transformed into General Patton, Doug Hanson had had an eclectic career: Geek Squad technician, Hyundai salesman, multi-level marketer for Dong Nutraceuticals, and a short and unhappy stint in the Coast Guard that ended with a dishonorable discharge.

His website, TRUAMERICANPATRIOT, had been an unexpected success. While collecting unemployment from the Hyundai gig, Doug was trying to make a little off-the-books cash by doing some online marketing. He held no particular political beliefs. However, from an advertising perspective, he realized it was better to appeal to the right. Conservatives lived in constant fear of race riots, civil wars, and the apocalypse, and were eager to buy products aimed at surviving catastrophes. They also tended to be elderly, happily ordering anything that might ease their ailments, regardless of how outlandish the claims. Right-wing pundits had figured it out. Glenn Beck sold gold and apocalypse survival kits. Sean Hannity hawked food insurance, pillows, and drugs designed to enhance prostate health.

TRUAMERICANPATRIOT initially pushed silver coins, powdered food, an online course to obtain a concealed carry permit, and various Dong products to aid digestion and erection difficulties. Doug, via his General Patton persona, promoted the site by spreading various conspiracy theories that would increase sales across the internet.

However, Corona was the big payday. When he repositioned Dong zinc tablets into a cure for the pandemic and added a cheap aquarium light that he claimed would kill the virus to the product line, profits increased sharply. Ultimately, he knew the government would shut him down, but they were so busy fighting the disaster that he anticipated it would take months, if not years. By then, cash would be siphoned to offshore accounts and the enterprise bankrupted, perhaps later to emerge under a new name.

General Patton had also become a conservative star, with a backlog of organizations anxious to pay him twenty thousand dollars to deliver speeches featuring the latest deep-state propaganda—the weirder, the better. His assertion that President Obama and Elizabeth Warren had run Washington, DC's biggest call girl ring received millions of views, as had a story he wrote claiming Jeff Bezos's Muslim butler was a eunuch that served him human flesh once a month. However, he regretted taking the cruise gig. This pandemic was the real thing, and he was anxious to get off the damn ship and to the log home he'd recently purchased in a remote part of Idaho.

Luckily, he had figured out a way to make a profit off of this situation. He had all but written off the ten thousand the knuckleheads in Santa Pulmo owed him, which wasn't too concerning because his cost of goods on the pills and lights was less than two hundred dollars. But using them to escape the ship allowed him to double his profits. He'd convinced the Chachi guy and the Fox News chick to each give him ten grand to get them off the boat. He found a crew member amenable to opening an emergency door at the rear of the Viva in exchange for letting him join them, and at midnight, the four were waiting for Danno and Pugs. He wasn't thrilled about climbing down the rocking rope ladder to sea level but was hoping for a big rescue craft that would make the escape easier.

~

Pugs and Danno were running late. The Avon rubber raft had a slow leak, and they had scrambled to find a pump to make it seaworthy. When they finally managed to start the ancient twelve-horse Mercury, it belched inky smoke, clanging as if a piston might shoot out the cowl. Examining the small craft, Danno yelled, "Jesus, how will we fit four more people in here? I don't think we should take this thing out in the ocean."

"It will be fine," Pugs said. "You can't sink a raft. People can sit on the sides. Besides, it's not that far out."

Neither had any experience piloting a boat, and they hit the waves sideways, filling the Avon with several inches of water. They saw General Patton swinging a flashlight back and forth as they veered to the rear of the Viva. The raft sat so low on the water that there was a six-foot gap to the bottom of the ladder.

"I thought you had a boat," Scott Baio yelled at General Patton. "That looks like something kids play with in a wading pool."

"Goddamn idiots," General Patton muttered. He stared down at the raft, and then addressed the group. "Listen, this is all we've got. We're just going to get a little wet. If you don't want to come, then stay here and take your chances with the snakes and the plague."

He climbed down to the bottom rung and dropped into the cold water, thankful for his Coast Guard training as Danno helped him in. Pugs had trouble holding the raft in position and smashed Scott Baio against the Viva, slicing open his forehead. Kaylee screamed that she couldn't swim, and Danno leapt in to help. When they were fully loaded, the raft was barely above water level.

"We're going to drown in this thing," Kaylee screamed.

General Patton was busy surveying the group, contemplating how many he'd have to throw overboard to keep the raft afloat.

~

SEDGE FRAWLEY HAD FALLEN asleep in front of the campfire, head propped on a sand pillow, when Dickie shook him awake. "Sedge, I think it's starting." He pointed at the swinging lights and the raft docking at the back of the Viva. The two were members of Duke's Clan: the right-wing militia Sedge had formed a few years earlier to protect Santa Pulmo from brown hoards and socialists.

The six members of the makeshift army normally congregated at Sedge's bar, Duke's, for weekly meetings. Patrons assumed the establishment was named in homage to the famous surfer, but members knew that Sedge secretly christened the rundown tavern after his personal hero, David Duke. Duke's Clan was required to wear their uniforms to meetings: antique Hawaiian shirts purchased on eBay. Sedge had sewn epaulets onto his shirt and ordered the militia to call him "Colonel," though behind his back, the men of Duke's Clan laughingly referred to him as Colonel Sanders or Colonel Klink.

The Santa Pulmo area was sleepy, and there had never been a need for a militia, but Duke's Clan enjoyed getting together to swap racist videos, shoot cans, play pretend army in the field behind the bar, and enjoy the free Pabst that Sedge provided.

However, the arrival of the Viva had given them a purpose. "That boat is chock full of Kung Fu virus, and we can't allow those people on our soil," Sedge had announced at the last meeting. "They might be planning an invasion that will start right here in Santa Pulmo. We're going to need twenty-four-hour-a-day surveillance from a beach outpost to stop them."

Since all of Duke's Clan were unemployed or on some kind of government assistance—and especially after Sedge had pledged to keep the garrison stocked with beer—everyone agreed to participate in the military exercise. Sitting around on a beach pounding brew seemed like good duty. Sedge also called into service the Duke's Clan navy, which consisted of Bobby Ulrich's seventeen-foot Boston Whaler, in case they needed to do battle at sea.

Sedge and Dickie were manning the ten p.m. to five a.m. shift, and by midnight they had consumed a cold pack when Dickie yelled at Sedge.

"Whaa," Sedge said groggily.

"The invasion. Look at the ship." Dickie pointed at the ocean. They spotted lights at the back of the vessel and passengers boarding a small craft.

"That's it," Sedge yelled, jumping up. "Battle stations." He grabbed the AR-15 leaning against a log, and the two sprinted toward the boat. Dickie had no experience piloting a watercraft and smashed the bow into the waves, tossing Sedge crossways. He lost his grip on the gun, nearly dropping it into the sea, and while grasping for it, his fingers squeezed the trigger. The weapon erupted, first blowing a hole in the front of the Whaler, and then sending a hail of bullets in the direction of the Viva. Sedge checked the bullet hole to make sure it wouldn't sink the craft and yelled at Dickie to cut off the raft, which was heading toward a closer shoreline.

The raft was making slow progress, the group screaming every time a wave washed over them, when they heard the gunfire. "Jesus Christ, someone's shooting at us," Scott Baio screamed.

"Faster, get to shore," General Patton yelled at Pugs.

"This is as fast as we can go with all these people," he replied as a four-foot wave swept over them and the drenched motor began to gasp.

"We're too heavy," General Patton yelled, as he shoved an unsuspecting Scott Baio and the Viva crewmember off the side of the raft.

~

On board the cruise liner, the captain, unsure of what was happening, called the Santa Pulmo police department to report gunplay, then notified the crew to initiate pirate protocol.

One of the stray bullets struck Yancey Felding's deck, lodging below his porthole. Yancey, a retired Marine and Vice President of Americans for Morality, was already in a foul mood. He'd saved for this cruise for two years only to have it decimated, his friends dead or sick due to the Chinese flu. He was sick and tired of soggy tuna sandwiches and living in a tiny cabin that smelled like ass. Now someone was shooting at him! Never a man to go anywhere unarmed, he grabbed his suitcase, pulling apart the false bottom to reveal the hidden Walther PPQ. He crawled to the deck, taking cover behind a teak table. A skiff was heading toward the ship, a man tottering in the front with a rifle. Yancey rose to a comfortable shooting stance and began firing. "Come and get it, asshole," he muttered, emptying his clip.

When the gunfire exploded from the Viva, Sedge realized he had made a serious misjudgment. He should have assumed the ship would be heavily armed and attempt to protect the invasion parties. He was yelling at Dickie to turn around when a bullet grazed his right shoulder. He spun and fell to the deck, which was covered in five inches of water. Another shot hit the engine, which exploded into flames. Dickie screeched and leapt off the craft, paddling hard for shore.

Scott Baio, disoriented in the black water, saw the boat lit up by the burning engine. He kicked hard toward it, grabbed the side, and grunted as he pulled himself up. "Chachi," Sedge moaned, looking up to see his childhood idol looming over him, figuring he must be dead.

~

Even with two fewer occupants, the raft was making slow progress. Pugs was concerned the sputtering motor would freeze up at any moment. Plus, he was pissed! *Scott Baio is an American treasure. He shouldn't be treated that way*. Bracing his back against the side of the raft, he kicked upward, catching General Patton in the chest and catapulting him backward into the water. The craft immediately picked up speed, leaving the screaming man flailing in the waves.

General Patton, the wind knocked out of him, struggled to gain his breath. The raft had disappeared in the dark, so he dog paddled toward the Whaler, a glow still emitting from the burning motor. Gasping, he crawled over the side. He saw Sedge moaning on the deck, the AR-15 lying three feet away. As he pulled himself into the boat, Scott Baio moved toward him from the rear, swinging an oar. General Patton flipped backward into the water as wood smashed into his chest.

~

A thousand feet away, the left tube completely flat, the group huddled against one side, the raft on its last legs when it reached the bank. Pugs could see flashing police lights on the road and forms with flashlights moving down the beach. "Quick, this way," he yelled, grabbing Kaylee's hand as the three ran in the opposite direction.

When a soggy General Patton washed onto the bank, he was greeted with a searchlight in his bleeding face. Several police officers carrying shotguns yelled at him to lie flat, and he was handcuffed.

Scott Baio rowed the burning craft to shore, and an ambulance was called for Sedge. Baio sat on a log as Officer Kathy Best applied a band-aid to the cut on his forehead, amazed to be touching one of her childhood crushes.

Scott Baio pointed at General Patton. "That's the guy that tried to kill us."

She looked down on General Patton, who was still lying face down in the sand. "You assaulted Scott Baio? Jesus. What's wrong with you?"

The police found Dickie on the beach and had him in handcuffs. Officer Best walked Dickie and General Patton to her car, roughly pushing them into the backseat.

"Where are you taking us?" General Patton asked.

"Jail. You'll be there a while. Maybe weeks or months. The courts aren't working very well due to the virus."

"But I didn't do anything," General Patton protested. "I was just trying to get off that damn ship."

"That's justification for attacking Scott Baio? And firing an automatic weapon at the ship? You could have killed dozens of people. My guess is they will charge you with attempted murder. There are probably some really serious charges for crimes committed at sea."

"I didn't fire the gun," General Patton yelled, throwing an elbow into Dickie. "It must have been this guy, or the wounded dude. I don't even know these people."

"Oh, Kathy, c'mon," Dickie cried, having spent many nights in the back of Officer Best's vehicle. "We can't go to that jail. Most of the people in there are infected. I have asthma. And diabetes. And gout. If I get the China flu, it could kill me."

"Should have thought of that before you started shooting," Officer Best said. "The detectives will sort it all out, but you're both going to be locked up. If anyone on the ship was injured, you will be in real trouble."

"Oh, please, not the jail," Dickie whimpered. "I don't want to catch the Corona."

Two hours later, General Patton and Dickie were sharing a holding cell, waiting to be transported to the county lockup. General Patton had hoped asserting his fame might help him get released, but when he explained who he was, the Sergeant, an African American, had replied angrily, "You're the guy that called President Obama a pimp?"

Another masked officer came to the cell and handed them each a small package wrapped in plastic. "You're going to want to wear this when you get to county lockup. The place is a mess."

General Patton pulled out the paper mask, embossed with *United Painting Supplies* on the bottom. "This isn't a medical-grade mask," he protested. "It's for house painters."

"Sorry, but there's a shortage. Beggars, or should I say criminals, can't be choosers. Besides, where you're going, it won't really matter. The jail is a real Covid hotspot."

General Patton fumed in frustration, visualizing his revenge on those idiots Danno and Pugs, and maybe even that damn Scott Baio. "Fucking Chachi," he muttered. "And fuck you, Viva Las Vegas."

Verse VIII
LEATHERHEAD

THOUGH HE HAD ONLY been four years old, Ruben remembered the day it all changed. He was asleep when his father, Ben, nudged into the little bed, folding his long skinny body into a cocoon around his son, awash with the mélange of smells Ruben associated with his father: motor oil, the final gasps of Aramis applied that morning, a tang of bourbon, and the less pleasant funk of Marlborough's.

Ben was gone Monday through Thursday, a traveling salesman hawking Gilbarco gas pumps to men in steel-toed boots. On Thursday night, he would creep into the house, careful not to wake his wife, Bridgette, who would raise holy hell at the fact her husband had beelined for the bar instead of returning to his family when he hit town. Ben claimed it was a requirement of the job; he needed to stop at the office and update everyone on the week's sales, which, of course, meant a beer at The Empire Bar after work. "I'm out there by myself all week. It's important I keep good relationships with the boss and the guys in the shop."

Of course, it was never just one beer, and Ben would stagger in around midnight, stopping to gaze at his sleeping son, often crawling next to him to give him a hug, intent on being the kind of father he had never had. "Hey, boy," he would say as Ruben stirred awake. "Dad's home."

"Daddy," sleepy Ruben would murmur, luxuriating in the tattooed arm encircling him.

"I missed you, Ruben. We're going to have a great weekend. Lots of baseball." With a final caress to his son's head, Ben would pad into the master bedroom to face his wife's wrath.

But on the night it all changed, he was more inebriated than usual, a long-ashed cigarette dangling from his right hand as he tripped into the bedroom. When he lay down next to Ruben, he passed out, unconsciously flinging an arm over his son's tiny body, sending the butt flying. He didn't know the blanket covering the boy had been the subject of a recall. The blend of cheap cotton and woven acrylic, treated with a potpourri of chemicals designed to make it stain resistant erupted like Sterno when the ash hit. Ruben awoke to molten fabric burning into his face and arms.

When Ben heard his son's cries, he drunkenly assumed it was another nightmare courtesy of his time in Afghanistan. A screaming specter was hopping around the room, face and arms shooting yellow fire. *It's my old friend Eric come to haunt me again.* Ben had been the first to jump from the vehicle when he hit the mine, abandoning Eric in the rear as the fuel tank exploded. His pal jumped from the vehicle, living just long enough to fry in front of his friends. Ben and the other soldiers extinguished the flames, but Eric was reduced to charcoal, conscious just long enough to beg Ben to shoot him.

However, in the dreams, Eric never appeared in his house, especially not in his son's bedroom. Moreover, the burning form was tiny—too small to be Eric. Ben bolted up and looked around more carefully. *Why was Bridgette in the dream, and why was she screaming?* Ben realized he wasn't asleep. His son was on fire. Bridgette had Ruben on the ground, and Ben jumped up and pulled off his leather jacket to help douse the flames.

The next few hours were blurry as he quickly sobered up. They were in an ambulance with Ruben, his beautiful little face and body now a melted mass of fried skin and black blood. Even the doctors looked shocked and warned them to expect the worst. "It's serious, and even if he makes it through tonight, we won't really know for several days," they cautioned.

In the waiting room, Bridgette exploded on Ben, pummeling his chest and face. "You fucking drunk," she screamed. "You set your own son on fire."

Ben welcomed the beating, leaning into it, wishing his wife possessed the power to twist his neck and crush his skull. *He was cursed.* First his best friend, and now his son. An hour later, he abandoned Bridgette at the hospital, leaving her curled in a lime-green plastic chair weeping into clenched fists. It was time to do the right thing. He was a dangerous man that needed to be stopped.

Returning to the house, he descended the wooden stairs into the makeshift basement and pulled the 12-gauge Remington out of the worn canvas case—his father's old pheasant gun. His dad would be pleased the weapon was put to good use. Kind of a family tradition. Ben didn't hesitate as he loaded a single shell, placed the barrel where his neck and chin intersected, pointed toward heaven, and pulled the trigger.

~

RUBEN REFUSED TO LOOK in a mirror, despite constant affirmations from his mother. "You are a brilliant, caring, funny young man," she assured him. "People just need to get to know you to understand how beautiful you are."

Beautiful? Ruben frowned at his mom. It was impossible to explain how it felt when children shrieked and cowered at the sight of you. Adults were not much better, unable to hide their shock and revulsion.

Initially, they hoped for a breakthrough with plastic surgery, but after multiple excruciating operations, they gave up. Ruben never came out better, just horrific in a different way. The fire had torched his face all the way to his skull, and there was too little to work with—just a patchwork of grafted flesh.

“Someday we will have the technology to fix you,” his doctor tried to assure him. “It’s just not quite there yet.”

Bridgette found a small Catholic grade school for Ruben, assured by the nuns that he would receive the best possible care and kindness. They gathered the classmates together on his first day, introduced Ruben, explained his situation, and urged the kids to demonstrate Christ’s compassion toward their new friend.

Some did, but to most of them, Ruben was a monster or a freak to be ridiculed. The latter would follow him like Frankenstein’s villagers as he walked home, chanting, “LEATHERHEAD, LEATHERHEAD, LEATHERHEAD,” a nickname bestowed by a pitiless six-year-old.

Initially, Ruben dashed into the house, where his mom would find him sobbing in his room. But after a week of harassment, he decided to just ignore it, keep his head down, and walk with determination. He would put on his headphones to drown out the cruelty. Sometimes the kids would throw snowballs or rocks, and one afternoon when he walked into the kitchen with a deep gash on his cheek, his mother decided it was time to make a change.

“People in this town are just too damn stupid and mean,” she told her son as she bandaged his wound. “Let’s get a fresh start somewhere we’ve never been. Somewhere with friendlier folks.”

Ruben nodded in agreement, unconcerned with the pain. He’d been through much worse.

Money was not an issue. Though Bridgette insisted on living a reasonable lifestyle, they were wealthy. Pacifico Textiles, the blanket manufacturer, had given Ruben a massive settlement. Ben owned a two-million-dollar life insurance policy that luckily paid on suicides, and they received his military and Social Security benefits.

Bridgette read a story in *The New York Times*’ travel section about a town that sounded welcoming, the headline proclaiming: STEP BACK IN TIME IN THIS CHARMING BEACH COMMUNITY. When the school year ended, they packed up the Toyota and headed to Santa Pulmo.

They settled in a 1940s Spanish bungalow two blocks from the beach. Bridgette had been a high school science teacher and figured the best use of her talent was to homeschool Ruben. She didn't want to put him through more trauma and hoped that as he aged, he would be better able to withstand the fear and hate. In Santa Pulmo's temperate climate, she was able to set up a tiny outdoor classroom, complete with a blackboard and an actual school desk she found in a secondhand store.

Shortly after they moved into the house, Al, the UPS man, arrived daily with shipments from their last home. Al and Bridgette became acquainted as he went over and above the call of duty, helping Bridgette lug big boxes into cluttered rooms. They formed an immediate, easy relationship, and she told him all about Ruben.

One day, the boy burst around the corner, immersed in a solo game of Space Army. He blanched when he saw Al for the first time. Coming from Montana, this was the first time he had been so close to a black man. Plus, he was nervous about the shock newcomers experienced when they saw him.

Al showed no sign that anything was out of the ordinary and threw the boy a big smile. "Who's this fine young man?" he asked, taking a step toward Ruben.

Ruben was surprised. Nobody had ever "not noticed." Bridgette told him to introduce himself. "I'm Ruben," he said softly.

"Well, hello there, Ruben. I'm Al Marsh," he said, extending a hand. "The guy that's going to be bringing you big boxes full of good stuff. Maybe even some presents."

Ruben tentatively took Al's hand. He was nervous to touch anyone, afraid his scars would disgust people or that perhaps they'd fear he was contagious, but Al didn't seem to care. Ruben had never touched a black man before and marveled that the skin felt the same as a white person.

"That's a fine grip you have there," Al said, as he surveyed the NY Yankees baseball jersey Ruben was wearing. "Any chance you might be a baseball fan?" Al gave Ruben's chest a soft poke as he dropped to one knee, their faces close. "I'm a Mets man myself, but that shouldn't stop us from being friends, should it?" Ruben swooned at the attention, experiencing the surge of happiness he used to feel in his father's trajectory. "So, are you a good ball player."

Ruben nodded.

"What position?"

"Third base. Like A-Rod."

"Fine choice. I was gonna say you strike me like a third baseman. Perfect build for it. How old are you?"

"Seven."

"Seven!" Al exclaimed. "I would have taken you for a much older man, maybe even eight. Are you married?"

Ruben giggled. "No, silly. I can't get married until I'm old like you."

"That's a good plan." Al laughed. "Say, I happen to coach Little League, and next year, you'll be old enough to try out. Maybe even play on my team, since now you have an in with the coach. The local bookstore sponsors us. We're called The Wordstock Wizards, and we could use a third baseman. Especially one that plays like A-Rod. If you like, we can practice and get you ready. Go to the park and hit the ball around. Would you like that?"

Wide-eyed, Ruben looked back and forth from Al to his mother, ferociously nodding.

"Good," Al said. "You go play, and I'll see if I can work out the details with your mom."

"Bye, Al," Ruben yelled as he ran around the house.

Al waited until the boy had rounded the corner, and then turned to Bridgette. "I hope I didn't do the wrong thing there. I should have checked with you first, but he seemed so excited. Course, it occurs to me you might not be too keen on some stranger taking your child to the park. I wouldn't blame you. But I can provide references. I'm a daddy myself." He smiled.

"No, Al, it's wonderful. I really appreciate it. He misses his father and really craves male attention. Any attention, really. It's hard. People are afraid. It's easy to forget he's just a little boy."

"Afraid?" Al laughed. "What kind of person would be afraid of that cute kid?" Al's expression grew more serious. "Listen, I have a lifetime of experience dealing with people who make judgements or fear me because of the way *my* skin looks. Maybe I can help Ruben."

For her son's benefit, Bridgette limited her crying to late at night, muffled with a pillow. For the first time in a long while, she felt joyful tears. "Thank you, Al, that would be wonderful," she said, throwing her arms around his neck.

Al stiffened, but when Bridgette began to sob, repeating, "He's just a little boy…just a little boy," he melted into the hug.

~

AL QUICKLY BECAME RUBEN's best friend and surrogate father. The two also shared a love of pranks and jokes. Bridgette had never seen her son laugh like he did when he was around Al. Once or twice a week, after his shift ended, Al would take Ruben to the park to play ball. He introduced Bridgette and Ruben to his family. Bridgette and Al's wife, Jeannine, soon became close friends, the group often gathering for weekend barbecues. Al's daughters were a few years older than Ruben, and they assumed the role of big sisters.

Ruben was comfortable around the group but continued to resist going out in public, and when other people drew close in the park, he would get nervous and want to leave.

"Ruben, you can't live your life as a hermit. Have to get out in the world," Al counseled.

Ruben related the story of his classmates chasing him and calling him Leatherhead.

"Leatherhead!" Al said, smiling. "That's badass. I like it. Lot better than the names ignorant folks call me. Anyone ever call you Porky McFatboy?"

Ruben laughed and shook his head.

"See, that's a lot worse. I love Leatherhead. Can I borrow it? I'd like to tell my pals at UPS to start calling me that. Sounds like a nickname Bruce Willis might have in a movie."

"It's not badass. It's mean."

"What do you think it means?" Al asked.

"It's an ugly man. Like a monster."

"Well, those kids were wrong," Al said. "You're no monster."

The following Saturday afternoon, Al had promised to take Ruben to a movie matinee after practice, and when Ruben opened the door, Al unzipped his jacket to reveal a T-shirt emblazoned with LEATHERHEAD in big white letters. He handed Ruben a sack. "I got you one, too. Go put it on."

Ruben was confused. "People will make fun of us."

"I promise they won't. Just put it on. You'll see."

As they approached the Orpheum Theater, Al pointed at the marquee, which advertised "LEATHERHEADS—STARRING GEORGE CLOONEY."

"The movie is called *Leatherheads*?" Ruben yelled in surprise.

"Yep, and you know what a Leatherhead is?"

Ruben shook his head.

"It's an old-timey football player," Al said. "Back in the day when football first started, they used to wear leather helmets, and people called the players Leatherheads. They were tough dudes. A lot tougher than players now. So maybe those kids just meant that you're tough."

"No," Ruben giggled. "They were being mean."

"Yeah, probably, but if someone does call you a bad name, you should just assume you remind them of George Clooney, and they are jealous," Al said. "Or maybe they think you're English. Leatherhead is also a town in England. Just say, 'Blimey, mate, how'd you know I was from the old country?'"

"Al, they were making fun of me." Ruben protested.

“Okay, but don’t let the haters win. Think good thoughts. Leatherheads are tough.

The following year when Ruben joined the Wordstock Wizards, Al held a team meeting. “Being on a team is like joining a brotherhood,” Al said. “You’re all brothers here, and that means you are kind to everyone, and you also protect your brothers. Anyone that doesn’t do that—anyone that makes fun of other people—well, they won’t be on the Wizards for long.”

The boys welcomed Ruben—especially after they saw him play—and, as Al had hoped, they became pals. At the end of summer, Ruben surprised his mom by suggesting he should enroll in school for the fall term.

“Wow,” Bridgette said. “I think that would be wonderful, but you know there will still be some mean kids.”

“I know,” Ruben said, “But I’m a Leatherhead, and we’re tough. Plus, all the Wizards will be there. And the Marsh sisters. I’ll have a lot of friends at that school.”

“Then I think it’s a wonderful idea.”

Chester A. Arthur Grade School proved to be a much kinder environment for Ruben. As the months passed, he stopped being an oddity to his classmates, and his many friends made it clear that any insult to Ruben would be regarded as an affront to them. The Marsh sisters, three and four years his senior, also kept a protective eye on him.

His abilities on the baseball field also made him popular, as he ranked as the best athlete in his class. The trauma of the fire and subsequent surgeries had imbued him with a toughness and dedication that his coaches found amazing. By the time he was sixteen, he’d helped lead the high school baseball team to a state championship.

Ruben was finishing his senior year of high school when Corona came calling. When the town went into lockdown, he actually felt a tinge of relief, as if he'd been granted a respite from the future that frightened him. He was scheduled to enter college the following fall with a full-ride baseball scholarship to the University of Oregon. While he was thrilled at the opportunity to play ball in the Pac-12 and dreamt of it leading to a career in the Major Leagues, he was terrified at the thought of being jerked from his safe little bubble and thrown into a new community.

He spent his days on Zoom trying to complete his classes and running baseball drills on evenings and weekends. He was the rare individual that found freedom in wearing a mask. Suddenly, he could walk through public places without the fear of strangers staring or being shocked at the site of him. He'd inherited his mother's coal black hair, which he wore long to cover the scars on his neck, and his father's bright green eyes, which made for a striking presence in his black mask.

When The Lazy Owl reopened in the spring, Al and Ruben made it a regular Saturday morning destination after practice for coffee and scones. "Looks like they have a cutey working here," Al said, motioning at the counter as they waited six feet back. Despite having many friends, Ruben had never had the confidence to date. Still, Al and the Marsh sisters were constantly encouraging him to meet girls.

"How can you tell? These masks hide a lot. Just look at me. Maybe she's a monster," he held his hands up in a Frankenstein pose.

"I happen to think you're quite a handsome young man," Al said. "A lot of character. Something a bit mysterious and Clooney-esque about you."

When they reached the counter, Ruben understood what Al had seen. The girl looked to be about his age, with blonde hair that cascaded in thick knots down her back. A thin rosebush tattoo encircled her left arm, ending in flowers on her knuckles. She was adorned with a leather bracelet and an antique jade ring. Though a mask, color-coordinated with her mauve T-shirt, covered her face, Ruben was sure whatever was beneath was beautiful. He tried not to stare at her hazel eyes, her cheeks upturned as if perpetually smiling.

Al gave her their order. "I don't believe we've ever seen you around here. Are you new to the Owl?" he asked.

"Yep, just moved here with my folks," the girl said. "Covid refugees from LA. Started yesterday."

"Well, welcome to Santa Pulmo," Al replied. "I'm Al Marsh, and my friend here is the local baseball legend Ruben Harper." He held his elbow out for a Covid handshake. "We're regulars, so you'll be seeing a lot of us."

"Hi," she replied. "I'm Danni Elway. Always nice to meet a legend," she said in a tone Ruben prayed was flirtatious.

"Elway," Al said. "You moved into the house on Lewis Avenue?"

"How did you know that?" Danni asked.

"Al's a well-known stalker around town," Ruben joked. "Probably a good idea to get a restraining order against him right away."

"Don't listen to him," Al laughed. "He took a fastball to the noggin today. Now he's not quite right in the head. I work for UPS, and I recognize your last name. I delivered quite a few boxes to your house this week. I think you even answered the door once or twice."

"Oh yeah," she smiled. "I didn't recognize you out of uniform."

"Nobody looks better in brown than Al," Ruben quipped.

"Will you be going to school here?" Al asked.

"Yes, I start at Santa Pulmo State in the fall. I was supposed to go to San Diego State, but with Covid, my parents thought it would be safer for us to stay together, at least for this year."

"Well, hopefully with everyone getting vaccinated, you can go anywhere you like soon. But Santa Pulmo State is a fine school, and I know you will enjoy it. And what a coincidence. You and legendary Ruben are the same age," Al said as she handed him their order. "Be sure to let us know if you have any questions about our little town.

Ruben knows all the hot spots for people your age and would be happy to show you around once things open up."

Ruben was glad she couldn't see him blush under the mask.

They sat down at an outside table, Ruben directing them to the side of the patio where he was sure Danni couldn't see him when he pulled off his mask to eat. "Thanks for embarrassing me."

Al smiled. "I saw how you were looking at her. Just trying to help. I'm a pretty good matchmaker."

"Thanks, but there's no chance in hell she'd be interested in me."

"And how could you possibly know that?"

"Once I took off the mask, she'd run away screaming. I guarantee it."

"And if she did, you'd know she wasn't the one for you," Al said patiently. "But maybe, just maybe, she would look at you and smile. See the same thing a lot of us see when we look at you."

Ruben decided to take Al's advice and became one of The Lazy Owl's best customers, visiting almost every day, at least when Danni was working. He discovered that she took her break at four, so he would time his arrival so she could join him at "their table," an outdoor spot next to the Owl's little herb garden. He was careful to order iced tea with a straw, which he slid under his mask to sip.

"You know, I think it's safe to take off our masks when we're outdoors," Danni said on the first day.

"You're probably right, but I would hate to get you sick. I'm around the guys at baseball practice, and some of them aren't too careful. You can take yours off if you want, but just for safety's sake, I want to keep mine on."

Ruben became a rapt student of all things Danni. He learned that she had an affection for old concert T-shirts (usually tied at the waist), *Game of Thrones* trivia, sushi, caramel macchiatos, feminist literature, yoga, and Timothée Chalamet films. She spoke French, had run high school track, considered herself an expert Nintendo *Bravely Default II* player, and dreamt of travel and a career in international business. In the fresh air, away from the overwhelming aroma of coffee in the shop, Ruben would surreptitiously lean in to catch a whiff of her hair, which smelled of lavender—a sensory experience that shot directly to his groin.

Danni was a good listener, and he told her bits and pieces of his life story, absent of the most important part: the fire and his father's suicide. At night, he would lay in bed and try to come up with the best strategy to address the subject, but when he was with Danni, he couldn't bear to tell her the truth, fearing the minute she knew he was a "Leatherhead," everything would change.

By May, the country was celebrating the wide availability of vaccines. Ruben knew it was selfish to hope everyone would stay masked a bit longer, but he wanted a little more time. In early June, he and Al made their normal Saturday stop at the Owl.

"Hey, guys," Danni said, beaming. "Check this out." She pointed at her I'VE BEEN VACCINATED button. "Got Pfizered this morning. In three more weeks, I will be free."

"Congratulations," Al said. "You scored the Cadillac of vaccines. I'm a Moderna man myself. Had my second shot last Thursday. And the legendary Ruben had his first poke a week ago."

"You didn't mention that. That's terrific. Just think, pretty soon, we won't need to wear these." She pointed at her mask.

"I take it she doesn't know?" Al said, noticing how glum Ruben became when they sat down outside.

"Can't I just enjoy my last few days of being in love before she discovers I'm the Hunchback of Notre Dame?"

"Ruben, you're not being fair to either of you. Listen, I don't know whether Danni is the one. You're going to meet many women in the next few years. Probably fall in love a few times. Get your heart broken a time or two. That's how life works. But you must give people a chance to get to know you. Have some confidence that they'll see beyond the scars on your face."

Ruben avoided the Owl for the next few days but found himself longing for Danni. With Al's continued encouragement, he finally found the courage to go back in. "Wow, where have you been?" Danni asked, irritation in her voice.

"Can I tell you about it on your break? I'll meet you at our table."

She frowned at him, then nodded.

Ten minutes later, Danni sat down, sliding an iced tea toward him. "Two lemons, one sugar," she said, "just the way you like it, stranger. So, what's going on? Because I have to tell you, I'm not going to be in a relationship with someone who ignores me and disappears."

Ruben was thrilled at the idea they were in a relationship, but returned to the dread of why he was there. "I'm really sorry. I wasn't ignoring you. I've been thinking about you constantly, but I have something I need to tell you." He dropped his gaze to the table. Slowly, he related the story of the fire and the move to Santa Pulmo. Danni grabbed his hands as he detailed his father's death and the many years of rehab.

When Ruben finished, he slid the straw from the iced tea and placed it on the table, terrified of what was to come next.

"So," he whispered, "I guess maybe…" But he had no more words. It was time. He slowly pulled down his mask and took a sip from the cup, trying to act casual, but intent on watching Danni's expression as she saw him for the first time. He felt as if he might burst as she reached across the table to softly caress his face, embarrassed that his cheeks might be damp with tears.

"Hello, Ruben," she smiled, and rose from her seat to kiss her boyfriend.

Verse IX

DON'T FUCK WITH AL

AL WAS BLASTING A little "Love and Happiness," fingers drumming the wheel, singing ferocious a cappella with the good Reverend Green. Returning home from the Lowes near Paso Grande, he was looking forward to weekend gardening and some quality Zoom time with his daughters, both stuck in quarantine five hundred miles away.

Covid added an entirely new level of stress and urgency to his job, and Al was craving some downtime. He'd morphed from deliveryman into an essential—if not the most essential—part of people's lives. The masked man in brown delivering life's necessities. He'd long ago memorized this stretch of road during twice-daily journeys back and forth from the UPS warehouse to his route in Santa Pulmo. Among locals, it was a known speed trap, so he stayed in check. Still, he instinctively jolted when he saw the police car tucked into a grove of oaks, a man in uniform leaning on the hood pointing a radar gun. He relaxed when he confirmed his speed—sixty-two in a sixty-five MPH zone—inadvertently locking eyes with the officer as he passed.

Al thought he knew every cop in the area, but he didn't recognize this man. The police and UPS drivers tended to have a close relationship, since the workers in brown uniforms served as a kind of neighborhood patrol when the men and women in blue were overburdened. Every week, Al would call to report wrecks and suspicious activities: abandoned cars, graffiti, and broken windows in unoccupied houses.

The previous year, he'd received an award from the city for community service. He was delivering a package to a house on Clark Avenue when he heard screaming and crying from inside, a despondent voice threatening violence. Al called 911 and yelled into a window to assure the terrified woman and her kids that help was on the way. Her husband, brandishing a butcher knife, made an incoherent threat, but Al reasoned with him in a soothing baritone. An Iraq vet, he was all too familiar with the kind of visions that challenged sanity, especially under the influence of God-knows-what, and he found common ground with the man. By the time police arrived, the two ex-marines were sitting on the front porch. Al had talked him into abandoning the knife on the dining room table, and now had a thick arm around his shoulders, the man weeping bad dreams into Al's ample belly, his wife and children huddled on the curb.

When the police car lit up and tore onto the highway, Al hoped it would pass him en route to another call. However, it pulled within two car lengths and bleeped. Al pulled over, sighed, and glanced around his Prius, trying to calculate the correct reaction. The rules for a black man engaging with police were sketchy and cruel. An inadvertent move, even reaching for a wallet, was subject to deadly misinterpretation. Plus, there was the issue of the mask. *What was the correct protocol during Covid?* He'd worn one in the store, and it was hanging from the rear-view mirror, but would the police officer want him to have it on? He decided it best to just ask when he came to the window. His iPhone was in a holder on the front dash, and as a precaution, he reached up and turned the camera to video mode before taking the safest posture by placing both hands high on the wheel. He held that position until the cop tapped on the window, then moved one hand to roll it down.

"License and registration," he said mechanically. Al winced when he noticed he was not wearing a mask, wondering why it was a requirement for UPS but not the cops.

"Sure thing." Al motioned at the glove box. "Can I reach in there, and then to my rear pocket to get my license?"

"Do it slowly."

"Do you want me to put the mask on?" Al motioned at the rear-view mirror.

"No mask."

Al was surprised to see the officer was clad in a bulky bulletproof vest, a heavy belt dangling all manner of weapons. The Santa Pulmo police typically appeared relaxed, preferring community policing to military-style enforcement. "All cops should aspire to be Andy of Mayberry," he'd once heard the chief of police joke. Al handed the officer the documents and slid his hands back to the wheel. "Can I ask why you stopped me? I don't think I was speeding."

"Why don't you leave the *thinking* to me," the officer said sarcastically. "Stay right here," he ordered before returning to his car.

Al turned to face his phone. "Just got pulled over for no reason. I'm a rotund, balding, forty-five-year-old black man, dressed in Docker khakis and a yellow polo shirt, so I do not resemble a Blood or Crip. Driving a Toyota Prius, the world's least intimidating car, filled with planting soil and a couple succulents for my garden. Not a dead body or automatic weapon in sight. I was driving under the speed limit when this officer stopped me." He glanced up and saw the cop exit his car. "So, hope for the best."

The police officer approached the window. "Where have you been today?"

"Did a little shopping," Al said in his friendliest voice. "I don't think we've met. I'm Al Marsh. New to the force?"

The officer frowned and said nothing, stepping back to look at the rear of the car to look through the back windows.

"I've been driving a UPS route in Santa Pulmo for almost twenty years." Al yelled through the window, "So we'll probably run into each other. I know everyone in the department. Brett Johnson and I play golf. I was talking to Kathy Best yesterday. I called in an accident on Roblar Road."

"Do you think that working for UPS and the fact you know a few cops gives you some kind of special privilege?" the officer asked sarcastically.

"No, not at all. I just thought—"

"Like I said, leave the thinking to me," he interrupted. "Have you been drinking? Maybe had a few beers with lunch after you went shopping?"

"No. I don't really drink. Maybe a glass of wine every now and then."

"Heard that before. You guys all drink. You sure I wouldn't find a few empty Colt 45 cans back there?" he looked through the window at the backseat.

"Colt 45," Al chortled. "I think you've mistaken me for Billy Dee Williams."

"Step out of the car," the officer said angrily.

"Why do you need me to get out?" Al asked, knowing nothing good could come of that. "I wasn't speeding, I haven't been drinking, and I'd just like to know why you stopped me."

"I gave you a direct order to exit the vehicle," the police officer said. "Do you want to go to jail?"

"Listen, officer, I don't mean any offense." Al attempted to de-escalate the situation. "We're on the same side. Ask anyone on the force. We all get along."

"If you don't get out of the goddamn car, I will pull you out through the window."

"Well, I doubt you're that strong," Al joked bitterly. "I'm a pretty big boy." However, not wanting to make things worse, he began to open the door. The officer was already reaching for the handle, and with double force, it flew open.

What happened next was not exactly clear on the video, but it appeared that the door banged into the cop's knee. When Al was out, the enraged officer threw an arm into the side of his neck, then repeatedly slammed him face-first into the Prius.

Al grunted. “Motherfucker, what are you doing?” When he pulled back, his mouth smeared with blood, he yelled, “I’m not resisting. I’m not resisting,” as the cop roughly yanked his arms behind him and handcuffed him.

If you listen closely, you can hear the officer yell, “Go ahead and fight back so I can split open your black skull,” as he walked Al back to the police car and shoved him into the backseat.

~

Officer Kathy Best had just started her shift when she received the call for assistance. Derek Lane had just joined the Santa Pulmo police force the previous week, and this was the first time she answered a call with him. She’d met him a couple times at the station, unimpressed with his old-fashioned cop swagger. Too much time spent working on his body and not his mind. He’d relocated from Corpus Cali, where he’d served ten years on their notoriously corrupt police force. Kathy was surprised Santa Pulmo would hire someone from there but knew the department was short-staffed. People were not lining up to go into law enforcement.

She parked behind Derek’s cruiser and was shocked to see Al in the backseat, his split lip swelling, blood dripping down onto his shirt. “Al,” she shouted. “What happened?”

Al nodded at Derek. “Ask him.”

She swiveled to face Derek. “Why is he in cuffs?”

“Resisted arrest. Then he assaulted me.”

“Al,” she said. “What’s going on?”

“Check the video. My phone is on the holder on the dash.”

Derek flashed shock and turned to the Prius. Kathy rushed ahead of him and removed the phone, which was still recording. Derek reached for it, but she swatted back his hand, crouched down out of the bright sunlight, and watched the video.

"You son of a bitch," she said to Derek, and then walked back to the car. She removed Al's handcuffs and helped him out of the car. "Jesus, Al, I am so sorry. I'll drive you to the hospital."

"What are you doing?" Derek hollered. "He assaulted me. I'm taking him in."

"Are you insane?" she yelled at Derek. "You pull this kind of shit…now?"

She handed Al his cell phone. "I'm so sorry. I guarantee you the chief will hear about this."

"Not your fault," Al sighed. "Unfortunately, there's still a lot of *his type* around," he motioned at Derek. "Tell the chief that man doesn't belong in Santa Pulmo. I don't need to go to the hospital. I just want to go home." He crawled back into the Prius and raised a weary hand at Kathy before driving away.

"What the fuck is your problem?" Derek yelled at Kathy as the Prius disappeared. Chest puffing, he moved toward her.

"My problem?" Kathy hollered back, her right hand tracing the grip on her baton as she stood her ground. Derek might outweigh her by fifty pounds, but she was prepared to plant the club right in his racist nuts.

~

AL AND JEANNINE MARSH had been married for twenty-four years. They'd met in San Diego a few months before Al was discharged from the Marines and eloped after a whirlwind romance.

When they first discussed marriage, Al had warned her. "Listen, a white girl marries a black man and people you've never met will come out of the woodwork to offer up a little hate. Most white folk, and some brothers and sisters…they don't take kindly to Caucasians jumping race. Are you sure you want to go through that?"

Al was the love of her life, and Jeannine assured him it would be okay. However, she'd underestimated the challenges. She had become accustomed to *the looks*—squinty-eyed reactions that screamed slut, race traitor, and every now and then, even a hint of admiration or pity. She was most amazed at the number of people with no filter or sense of decency. People not ashamed to call her names. Sure, she expected it from the redneck contingent, but a well-dressed business executive or a dainty mother from her daughters' school might just as easily deliver a racist comment in more subtle language.

Jeannine's initial reaction was to shy away from crowds, preferring to socialize with their small group of friends. However, after her two beautiful coco-skinned girls were born, she understood the prejudice they would face and adopted a warrior's mentality, never shy to confront even the slightest insult. It often fell to Al to calm her down. "You can't let hateful folks fill you with anger, otherwise they win. Just ignore them."

"Or I could just punch them in their cracker mouths," she countered. "That would feel better."

Jeannine was especially affected by the death of Breonna Taylor. She could imagine one of her daughters, asleep in her apartment, when armed men burst through the door to murder her. Santa Pulmo was lily white, a little color around the edges provided by the Hispanic contingent that kept the machinery operating. Jeannine could count the black residents on both hands, but luckily, she found the mostly liberal community anxious to do the right thing, more racially obtuse than racist. When Black Lives Matter kicked in, there was plenty of enthusiasm, and Jeannine soon headed the committee that helped coordinate supportive messaging and assisted local organizations and city government improve their own diversity.

She was working in the kitchen when Al walked in and reached into the freezer to retrieve some ice for his swollen face. "What happened to you?" She asked, placing a palm under his chin.

"Oh, you know..." he said, shaking his head in disgust. "White cop meets black man, and fun ensues."

"A policeman did this to you?"

Al told her the story and showed her the video. "Now, please don't go making a big deal of this," he pleaded. "Next week, I'm going to set up a meeting with the chief to show her this, and I'll make sure the guy gets what's coming to him. But I don't want to be put in the center of anything. There's too much going on right now to add fuel to the fire."

When Al went outside to unload the car, Jeannine grabbed his phone, sent herself the video, and forwarded it to her friends and members of the BLM group. "See, even we have a problem in our perfect little community," she texted.

Three hours later, Al had finished planting the succulents and trimming the rosemary and was rolling the wheelbarrow into the garage when a news van from the local television station pulled into his driveway. Al recognized a masked Kaylee Johansson, the new news anchor. All of Santa Pulmo had been shocked when the former Fox personality left the limelight to work as a reporter at the little local station.

Kaylee, cameraman in tow, rushed toward him. "We're here with Al Marsh, a longtime Santa Pulmo resident, known to many of us as Al, the UPS Man. Al, we understand that you were the victim of a vicious racist attack by a Santa Pulmo policeman earlier today?"

Al grimaced. *How in the hell did she know?* He held a hand up in front of his face. "Kaylee, I'd prefer to handle this. I'm going to talk to Chief Whitmore about the incident on Monday. I don't want to be on television."

"Mr. Marsh, from the look of your face, you were obviously injured, and I know everyone wants to know the details," Kaylee said.

Al was about to politely decline further comment and hustle back into the house, when a police car pulled next to the van. Chief Whitmore and Mayor Wheeler jumped out, obviously alarmed at the sight of the news crew.

"Hey, Al," the mayor yelled, rushing to Al's side and grabbing his arm as he moved him toward the porch. "Any chance we could sit down and talk?"

Kaylee turned to Mayor Wheeler, intent on asking a question, but the three rushed into Al's house and shut the door as she was climbing the steps. "Jesus, Al," Chief Whitmore inspected Al's face. "Did that idiot Derek do this to you?"

"His temperament is better suited for a Klan rally," Al replied with a pained smile. "What is going on? The newswoman out front, you two here… How did the word get out so fast?"

"The video is all over the internet."

Al turned to Jeannine with a frown. "How in the hell…"

"Al, it's important. People need to know that police racism even happens here."

"I didn't want to turn this into some kind of online thing," Al said. "Chief, I was going to come to you next week so you could deal with the guy. People are already freaked out enough with Corona, and I don't want to create anymore tension."

"I appreciate that, Al. I am so sorry, and rest assured, I am going to take care of Derek. He'll be fired today, and I'm going to do everything I can to make sure that kind of bullshit doesn't happen again. We've got some special training lined up for the force."

"I'm offering apologies for the entire city," Mayor Wheeler added. "I feel terrible about this."

Al nodded. "Thanks."

"Hate to ask, but we could use your help to keep things in control. They've already scheduled a protest for tonight," Mayor Wheeler said. "A march through downtown. We'd like you to be there. Give an uplifting speech. The Chief and I are going to participate. I think a nice, controlled event to highlight the problem and show that we are addressing it is a good idea. Make it a community gathering."

Al sighed. Even though he knew this was a serious subject, the last thing in the world he wanted was to be the face of some kind of movement. He turned and glared at Jeannine, then turned back to Mayor Wheeler. "I'm not much of a speech giver, and I don't really want to be some kind of poster child."

"Al, we need you," the mayor pleaded. "Everyone in this town loves you, and they want to hear what happened, and that you're confident we're handling it. You're the one guy that can keep things calm."

Al nodded slowly, wishing he'd decided to stay home today.

~

SEDGE FRAWLEY WAS ENJOYING his third Pabst of the afternoon when he received the call. He knew it was a bad idea for a bar owner to consume his own inventory, but since Covid hit, there hadn't had much traffic at Duke's, and he increasingly found himself shitfaced by four in the afternoon. *Bars are for drinking*, he rationalized, *and if he didn't have customers getting drunk, he might as well fill in.*

The caller ID announced Rance Parlow, and Sedge perked up. Rance was the regional head of the Boogaloo Bois—the right-wing organization loosely affiliated with Sedge's militia, and Sedge was thrilled to hear from him. Sedge's group, Duke's Clan, seldom received any attention from leadership, and he knew bigger militias sometimes laughingly referred to them as The Daisy Dukes. Perhaps their courageous gun battle with the filthy Viva hoard had elevated their status.

"Rance," he answered brightly. "Great to hear from you."

"Are we secure?" Rance asked.

"Secure?" Sedge asked.

"IS THIS LINE SECURE?" Rance yelled impatiently.

"Uh, yeah," Sedge said, not knowing the answer. *Is Verizon secure?*

"Listen carefully," Rance ordered. "We're tracking a protest scheduled for tonight in Santa Pulmo. Our intelligence reveals that violent Antifa and Black Lives Matter members might crash the event, so we need your assistance."

"Yeah, I heard about the rally." Sedge felt a surge of adrenalin and pride. "My boys are ready to kick some ass."

"We don't need any ass kicking," Rance barked. "Right now, violence is a last resort. We just need to discredit them."

"Discredit? What do you mean?"

"I need you and some of your men to pretend to be Antifa. Dress up in black, wear masks, and do a little damage we can pin on them. Nothing too serious. Break a few windows. Spray paint ANTIFA RULES and BLM on a few buildings."

"But won't they do all that?" Sedge asked.

"Can't take the chance. Sometimes the little pussies just chant and carry signs," Rance answered. "Last week in Austin, they handed out donuts."

Sedge was confused. "Well, if they don't cause any damage, what do we care? Folks like donuts."

"Christ," Rance said in exasperation. "What is your problem? Do you know what Antifa stands for?"

"Anti-fascist?" Sedge asked. "Wait," a light went off in his head. "We're not fascists now, are we?"

"No, you fucking idiot," Rance yelled. "Antifa supports the bastard races…the coloreds, the spics, Jews, commies, socialists, and pedophiles. All the filthy liberal lowlifes. And we can't let these Black Lives Matter radicals take control."

"Sure," Sedge said, "nobody is more pro-white than me. The thing is, the guy the cop beat up is a good dude for a black fella," he said to Rance. "Al delivers here, and he and I get along. I don't want to hurt him."

"Jesus, what the hell is wrong with you?" Rance said. "Nobody said anything about hurting him. I just need you to discredit Antifa. We're at war. Right now, it's an information battle."

"Okay, you can count on me," Sedge said, anxious to impress Rance.

~

At five p.m., Chief Whitmore called a meeting of the six members of the Santa Pulmo police force, omitting just one employee, Derek

Lane, who she left on patrol. "I assume all of you saw what happened today to Al Marsh?"

The group mumbled angrily.

"And you know about the protest?"

More nods.

"So, I need everyone to work tonight. We don't want this thing spinning out of control. Just remember these are your friends and neighbors. They are upset. Tough times. Be kind. Stay masked, and hand out masks to anyone who needs them. I don't want this to be a super-spreader event. There's always the chance a few out-of-towners might show up to cause trouble. There is a little online chatter that Antifa might make an appearance, but we think it might have been sent out by some far-right groups. You all pretty much know everyone in town. Keep an eye out."

"What about Derek?" Officer Kathy Best asked. "Did you fire the bastard?"

Chief Whitmore frowned. "That's the other thing I wanted to talk to you all about. I called his union rep to let him know I was getting rid of Derek, and he told me if I terminated him, he would call all of you out on strike. I can't afford that right now."

"That's bullshit," Kathy said. "I wouldn't go on strike to support that asshole." The other officers shook their heads in agreement, a few murmuring, "Damn right."

"Would any of you strike if I get rid of Derek?" the chief asked.

Captain Brett Johnson, the highest-ranking officer under the chief, spoke up. "Our union rep lives two hundred miles away and visits us once a year. I don't give a damn what he says. I'm friends with Al, and he's one of the finest men I know. If you don't fire Derek, I'd be inclined to break both his legs and throw him out of town myself."

"Everyone agree?" Chief Whitmore asked, the group nodding. "Okay. Frank, can you find a cardboard box? Kathy, have dispatch call Derek back to the station?"

The group went into the locker room, pried the lock off Derek's locker, and shoved his belongings—which included a collection of mixed martial arts magazines, a jumbo-sized carton of BlueChews, a tube of Clearasil, a set of nunchucks, pills they assumed to be steroids, and ointment used to treat cold sores—into the tattered Amazon box. The cops were milling in the parking lot ten minutes later when Derek pulled in.

"Derek, you're fired," Chief Whitmore said as he crawled out of the car. "Here's your shit. I'll take the badge, gun, and car keys."

"What?" Derek puffed up. "That was a legitimate bust. She's the bitch that screwed it up," he motioned at Kathy.

"Derek, you're a Neanderthal that thinks it's okay to beat up people and call women bitches. I want your badge and gun. Take your smelly gym clothes, karate magazines, and dick and zit medications, and leave town."

"Screw you," Derek said. "The union is going to crucify you. You can't fire me, and there's no way I'm leaving town."

"If you don't surrender your weapon and badge right now, we're going to take it from you, and then we will lock you up for assault." The group moved a step closer, and Kathy pulled the taser from her belt. "If you don't leave Santa Pulmo within a week, we will haunt you. Stop you every day for questioning. Search your car. Bang you around a lot worse than you did Al. If you resist, because asshole hotheads like you always do, then you might really get hurt."

"Feel free to resist," Brett smiled, pulling out his nightstick.

"You can't threaten me," Derek screamed. "I'll sue."

"Threaten you?" The chief said, tilting her head in confusion. "Anyone hear me threaten this man?"

The group shook their heads. Kathy smiled. "I thought you were really sweet, Chief."

"Very supportive and professional," Brett added, as the rest of the officers nodded. "Derek might be having one of those steroid-induced psychotic episodes." He turned to the chief. "I probably should have mentioned it earlier, but I fear that Derek has some kind of addiction issue and is using illegal drugs. That would explain his frequent rages and the disgusting acne on his back."

Derek ripped off his badge and removed the gun belt. "Fuck you," he said, as he picked up the box and headed toward his car. Careening through the lot, he banked the Dodge Challenger to pepper the group with gravel as he fishtailed onto the street.

SEDGE FRAWLEY HAD RECRUITED Dickie and Bobby Ulrich to assist with tonight's mission, all three thrilled to have a real assignment from headquarters.

"Sedge," Dickie said when the task was explained, "how about we really make an impact. We could burn down Tipsy's Tavern and make it look like the anti-fi-fa-di did it."

"Jesus, Dickie, you just want to burn down Tipsy's because you're not allowed to drink there anymore ever since you puked all over the bar," Bobby said.

"We're not burning anything," Sedge barked. "Rance was clear about the assignment. Throw a few bricks through windows and do a little spray painting. I need you to go home and dress all in black. Bring ski masks and a can of red paint. Dickie, you can even wear that old army helmet you love so much. When everyone is marching downtown, you just run through really quick and break some windows and spray paint some Antifa and BLM crap on a few buildings."

"What about you?" Dickie asked.

"I'm going to head downtown and drop the bricks in piles so you can just hustle through and grab them. It would slow you down and look suspicious if you were carrying them. You park on Edison, then head toward the school. I will leave a pile on the east corner of the school in the alley. Take out a few windows, spray paint 'BLM' and 'ANTIFA' all over the place, then head across the street to the back of the courthouse and do the same thing. Then, run straight down the alley. I will drop another pile behind the Lazy Owl. You can hit a few of the businesses right there while everyone is a block away. I'll be waiting in my truck at the corner; you jump in, take off the disguises, and I'll drive you back to your car. In and out in ten minutes." The men nodded. Breaking windows seemed like something they could handle.

Two hours later, Sedge was in the alley loading bricks in a pile off the back of his Dodge Power Wagon. Suddenly, a laughing group came around the side of the school. Since it was a weekend, Sedge had assumed nobody would be in the area, but a half dozen masked children walked toward his truck. Mr. O'Donnell, the junior high history teacher, thought the rally would be a wonderful opportunity for the kids to see civic action in person and had invited the team to meet and walk to the event. When he saw Sedge unloading bricks, he veered in his direction.

"Thank God," he said, "they're finally going to repair those steps." He motioned at the crumbling brick staircase at the back door of the school. "I told them it wasn't safe, but with all the cutbacks, plus Covid, it's tough to get anything done. I'm happy to see they're fixing it. Kids, help this nice man unload these bricks." He motioned at the group, and three boys jumped in to empty the load. "Thanks so much for doing this," he said to Sedge.

Sedge nodded, frozen in place. After the group departed, he walked to the school to examine the steps, which looked like they should be condemned. In fact, the entire building appeared sorely neglected, one wall covered with graffiti that dated back almost a decade, the windows on the second story cracked and taped in place. The door was peeling and caving in due to dry rot. He had no idea the place was in such rough shape.

Sedge remembered attending this school forty-five years earlier, when it was new and the pride of the community. In those days the citizens of Santa Pulmo, many of them war vets, had taken enormous civic pride in their town, happy to support schools, parks, and good streets. Hundreds of people had turned out for a ribbon-cutting ceremony to open the building, and twelve-year-old Sedge had been there with his father.

His dad was so delighted you would have thought he owned the building. "You should have seen the awful place where I went to school. Drafty, falling down, even had rats. I'm so happy you get to go to such a great place."

The previous year, Sedge had voted against the school bond issue, figuring any tax was an assault on patriotism, and was thrilled when it was defeated, but now he realized they should have passed it. Vandalizing this place seemed akin to kicking a man when he was down. *It was easy for Rance to give orders to destroy a town he didn't live in*, Sedge figured.

Sedge had returned to his truck when he saw Dickie and Bobby running down the alley. As directed, the two were dressed in black. Bobby was wearing a ski mask, but Dickie appeared to have cut eyeholes into one of the legs from a pair of pantyhose, which pulled tight on his face with ghoulish effect. When they stopped in front of Sedge, Dickie spewed the deep bark of long Covid cough, as he pulled up the mask and wheezed for oxygen.

"Sedge, what are you doing here?" Bobby asked.

"It's off," Sedge answered. "It doesn't make any sense to vandalize our own town."

"Rance ain't gonna like that."

"Jesus, Sedge, at least let me break the windows out of Tipsy's," Dickie pleaded.

"Nah, and screw Rance," Sedge said. "Give a hand with these bricks. I'm donating them to the school to fix the steps. It'll be good publicity for the bar."

"Didn't you steal these from the new CVS store they're building?" Dickie asked.

"Yeah, but the school needs them more than they do," Sedge said, considering whether this donation might qualify for a tax deduction.

After unloading the bricks, Dickie and Bobby pulled off their disguises, and the three drove to the town square, standing at the corner to watch the gathering. Al Marsh had mounted the library steps and was just finishing a speech to the masked crowd of a couple hundred, encouraging everyone to "be kind."

"Well, lookee there," Dickie said. "They're handing out free ice cream. This is my kind of protest," he said as he headed to the booth.

Sedge sensed the crowd's electricity, a happy vibration from humans that had spent months in isolation, now anxious to greet each other with excessive kindness. He watched masked people yell greetings to friends, then stop to deliver the Covid bow, while excitedly catching up six feet apart. It occurred to him this was the kind of town he had always wanted to live in.

At the opposite side of the square, Derek Lane was also observing the festivities but with a much different reaction. He watched Al deliver his happy little kumbaya speech, seething when he described the "racist bad apples" that needed to be purged from law enforcement before saying, "But now we need to treat each other with love."

Love.

This black bastard had gotten him fired. Nothing loving about that. And that bitch police chief was standing ten feet from Al.

Derek tingled with the thought of retribution. Al traveled some lonely back roads in his UPS truck. Almost anything could happen. And the chief…

We will see how tough you are when you aren't surrounded by six other cops.

Verse X

COLLARED

Father John often flashed back to the first assault. Six years earlier, he had traveled to New York, an annual trip with his sister for a weekend of Broadway shows and Italian food, when he was confronted outside the Marriott Marquis in Times Square.

"Pedophile," the man hollered, launching a missile of phlegm from his angry lips. Father John jerked back to avoid being splattered in the face, the slimy gob spreading yellow on the lapel of his black suitcoat. The attacker, bald and egg-shaped, wearing a leather-sleeved jacket sporting Yankees logos, reared back as if he might expel another loogie, screaming, "You're all perverts and rapists."

Father John put a protective arm up for his sister, gently pushing in front of her, while he considered his options. The man outweighed him by at least forty pounds, but Father John had the height advantage and felt certain he could put him down. He'd spent many afternoons in a Taekwondo studio, the classes a gift from the parishioner who owned the dojo, and while he went for exercise and the spiritual aspects more than defensive training, muscle memory pushed him into a fight stance. His attacker was a wide and out-of-shape target, his fat face cherry with rage, as if he might drop from a cardiac arrest on his own. Father John considered the image of a Catholic priest drop-kicking a man to the pavement. It would be captured on the dozens of videos being shot as the crowd ripped out their phones, and he could envision it going viral. Some would question why a man who professionally advocated peace and turning the other cheek had taken the time to earn a black belt and didn't hesitate to get into street fights. While it was reasonable to defend himself, the priesthood didn't need additional attention or controversy.

Arms raised in a defensive posture as the man continued to berate him, he searched the crowd for help. There was a time when a public assault on a priest would elicit near riotous assistance. But as he looked at the faces of those around him, no one seemed anxious to defend the holy man. In fact, a few people were smirking, leaving John to wonder if they might join in against him.

"Hey, hey, hey," he said in a calm voice. "Calm down. Let's talk."

"One of you perverts raped my brother," the man screamed, raising his fists. "He killed himself because of it." The crowd moaned in sympathy and disgust, and Father John realized the situation was deteriorating.

That's when Batman stepped in to save the day.

Looming large in a vinyl Batman suit, Sebastien Gonzalez was soliciting tourists to have their photos taken when he saw the attack. Mickey Mouse, Luigi Mario, Cinderella, and a nearly naked woman (her skin stained blue with strips of copper-colored plastic covering nipples and genitals) stood by, but Sebastien, who had grown up in the church in Guadalajara and was a proud former altar boy, was outraged to see a padre being abused. Pushing through the crowd, he grabbed the fat man by the back of his jacket and propelled him five feet forward, where he splayed across the sidewalk. The man swiveled, shocked and confused to see the Caped Crusader standing above him. "Don't you ever touch a priest," Batman warned with a clenched fist. The man's wife helped him up, and the two scampered away toward Eighth Avenue.

Father John thanked Sebastien as his sister wiped the spittle off his coat, depositing the wad of Kleenex in a waste can shaped like Donald Duck, as the tourist paparazzi continued to photograph the three. Sebastian refused the ten dollars Father John attempted to give him—I *could never take money from a padre*—but happily posed with the two for a picture.

That night Father John emailed Bishop Freemont about the episode. "Suddenly, they hate us," he wrote. Public respect and safety had always been one of the perks of wearing a religious collar that Father John enjoyed most. He might have to endure a lifetime of celibacy, near-poverty, and constant three a.m. phone calls to assist someone in need, but in return, he could expect respectful smiles and greetings from strangers, prime seating on public transportation, elevator doors being happily held open, and an occasional check discretely picked up in a restaurant by a person of faith.

Bishop Freemont confirmed his fear. "We've had reports of priests being assaulted all over the country," he said. "Be careful. In Phoenix, someone knocked on the rectory door at St. Andrews, and when Monsignor Desmond answered the door, they punched him in the face and broke his nose. A priest was shot in Barcelona, though we suspect some justification for that one."

Father John sensed a transformation in his own parish in Santa Pulmo. The barrage of abuse claims against priests denigrated the church and made the calling look like a coven of deviants. Attendance and donations had plummeted at Holy Rosary, with people unwilling to lend financial support to an organization that needed the money for legal fees and sexual abuse settlements. It became impossible to recruit altar boys and girls, and the youth group was disbanded, parents afraid to leave their children alone in a room with a priest. Now wizened old men appropriately devoid of sexuality stood on the alter during mass to assist him.

Father John had once occupied a position of respect in Santa Pulmo, an honored addition to community events, but those invitations were no longer proffered. Now he only received occasional dinner offers from widows who might welcome carnal contact and a standing invitation to the Catholic Men's Club monthly luncheon, which had morphed into an old white man's conservative bitch session, replete with racist and sexist undertones that made him cringe. At the last meeting, there had been serious discussion of discontinuing the food bank that served the immigrant community. "I don't think we should be encouraging these criminals by feeding them," Len Feldman argued, stuffing his face with a tomato most likely picked by the target of his ire.

Every few months, Father John would take a long weekend and make the three-hour drive to San Francisco. He'd discovered an inexpensive motel near Fisherman's Wharf and enjoyed all-day walks exploring the city. He started leaving his clerical collar in his room, preferring to just be an anonymous middle-aged age man. On Saturday, he might be lucky enough to obtain a half-priced matinee ticket for the theater, followed by pasta in North Beach and the requisite trip to City Lights Bookstore to stock up on reading material. While he frequented Wordstock, the bookstore in Santa Pulmo, he had to be selective about his choices for fear of creating local controversy if he was seen purchasing "lefty or provocative literature."

Father John was a devoted liberal, confident that Jesus would be anti-war, pro-immigration, an environmentalist, and against the accumulation of massive wealth. But he also didn't believe in publicizing his opinions for fear of alienating someone seeking a relationship with God. At City Lights, he felt free to peruse every section of the store, unafraid to read books that might challenge his own beliefs, sometimes even attending readings by atheists and others that held disdain for the church.

He sometimes ended the night with a scotch served neat—single malt if he was feeling decadent—at Tosca, always sitting at the end of the bar to silently observe the kind of festivities he'd never personally experienced. When he wore the collar, this was problematic; people assuming a priest who imbibed even one cocktail must secretly be a raging alcoholic, wandering the rectory late at night, yelling at Satan in a drunken fog while chugging holy wine.

He also understood that if his congregation knew of his San Francisco sojourns, many would assume nefarious intent. Perhaps their priest was frequenting prostitutes or the porn shops that lined the Tenderloin, or worse, dressing up in women's clothing and visiting a boyfriend. They would find it difficult to accept that Father John was as chaste as presented and only seeking temporary respite from the drudgery of his daily duties.

Over the years, sitting in the confines of the tiny confessional, he'd heard every gory detail of the compulsions, addictions, and life-altering mistakes that destroyed people: alcoholics and addicts who abandoned health and family for a momentary high, thieves and cheats who took advantage of the most vulnerable, the pain of a secret existence, the consequences of choosing degrading lifestyles, lives spent paying the toll for abusive parents and often passing on that mental illness.

His personal knowledge of sin was based on observation and not action. His sex drive was minimal; his occasional desires easily squelched with a quick round of self-pleasure. He had no attraction to men, and while he enjoyed the company of females, on the rare occasion when a woman chose to flirt with him, he was flattered, but unmoved. While he didn't object to a quick toke from a joint, anything stronger held no appeal. He enjoyed the buzz of a couple glasses of wine or a cocktail, but could honestly say he'd never been drunk to the point of losing control. Sinning was so often an act of excesses, and he was content with a simple life.

But that was putting him at odds with the church he loved. He'd always been disturbed by the pomp of Catholic hierarchy. He doubted that Jesus would look kindly on his soldiers decked out in ornate garments and living in palaces. The church was a gold-clad international conglomerate seeking relevance as opposed to a haven of enlightenment and redemption. So, he opted to ignore the outside world and concentrate instead on the needs of his parish. But when a worldwide epidemic came calling at Holy Rosary, he was pulled into controversy.

It began when he followed state statutes forcing him to suspend church services during the most severe days of Covid. The overly faithful were outraged, accusing Father John of being an agent of the state. "This entire Covid thing is bullshit," Len Feldman screamed at him. "And you are a fool for buying into it. You can't shut down the church because of a little China flu."

One morning, he awoke to find picketers hurling insults in front of the rectory, as if protesting a dictator. He was subjected to threatening voicemails and emails. He considered inviting the irate to help him minister to victims of the horrible disease they didn't believe in so they could see the truth. There was something particularly evil about an illness that forbid human contact during the final gasps of life.

Father John was overjoyed when the first Covid vaccination was released and encouraged his flock to stay masked and get poked, which once again drew the ire of conservative parishioners. The complaints and threats ratcheted up, one anonymous note threatening to "burn down the rectory with Father John in it." The final straw came in a phone call from Bishop Freemont.

"John, I'm getting a lot of calls. You need to quit talking about masks and vaccines. It's riling people up."

"Isn't it part of my job to protect the parish?" Father John protested. "I'm sick and tired of burying people that didn't need to die."

"We can't take a position on this," the bishop said sternly. "The church doesn't play politics."

"That isn't true. The church has always been steeped in politics. But there is nothing political about this. It's a public health emergency, and people need our guidance. Would you advise people not to get vaccinated for polio or measles if it offended their politics? Besides, the sooner people are healthy, the sooner we can get back to regular services."

"Stay out of it," the bishop barked, then softened his tone. They both knew the church could not afford to lose priests. "Listen, John, I know you've been under a lot of pressure. Take a week off.

I'll send Father Leo down to handle things while you get your head on straight." Father John fought the temptation to tell the bishop he needed to remove *his* head from his ass, but quietly concurred. Perhaps a break was in order.

The return to San Francisco was fast with so little traffic on the road, and the empty motel seemed overjoyed to have his business. San Francisco during Corona was eerie, like an abandoned city in one of those end-of-the-world movies, with desolate streets populated with homeless roaming zombie-like. The theaters were closed, but Father John was excited to discover his favorite restaurant was open with outdoor seating, and he enjoyed long meals, lingering over espresso while perusing the news on his phone. He wandered the neighborhoods but sensed there had been some profound change in the world that he could not quite decipher.

Nothing seemed real anymore. The ministry to which he had dedicated his life was political, and perhaps even criminal. His pride and patriotism of being an American were displaced by distrust and fear of the government and a portion of the population anchored in cruelty. The end of days was no longer just a science fiction concept, and for the first time, he was not quite sure he had been playing for the right team.

Park Dojo. Near Union Street, he saw the sign and stopped to gaze in the window. It was a simple matted room found in every karate training facility. A slight but sturdy Asian man, dressed in an orange karategi, was performing perfect katas. Father John watched him, admiring his controlled form, a perfect dance. The man's movements increased in speed and precision, and Father John was mesmerized as he seemed to levitate, catapulting through the air to elegantly flow into a roll, popping up across the room only to fall and rotate on the mat, springing up ten feet away. It reminded Father John of the special effects in *Crouching Dragon* or a John Wick movie, except this was a man of flesh and blood so skilled he seemed to defy gravity. After a couple minutes, he stopped, smiled at Father John, and motioned at him to come in.

They greeted each other with the traditional bow that had supplanted the handshake in the Covid world but which was standard practice in the dojo. The man introduced himself as Seo-jun Park. "You are interested in karate?"

"Yes," Father John said. "I have been studying Taekwondo for many years, but I certainly don't move like you. I've never seen anything like it. Would it be possible to train a little with you? Or even just observe. It's miraculous. I didn't think a human could move that way."

Seo-jun laughed. "I myself am constantly amazed by what the human body is capable of. Sometimes, one needs to put aside old attitudes and perceptions, and you might surprise yourself. And as far as training with me…well, you would need to get in line behind all these other students." He made a sweeping gesture to the empty room, then threw Father John a comical look. "Guess you're next. Covid is not good for my business, and I have had to cancel most of my classes, though hopefully Pfizer is fixing that problem. My class is not for a couple hours, and I would be happy to work with you."

He led Father John into a tiny locker room and gave him a clean but worn karategi to change into. For the next two hours, the two trained, but not in any way that Father John had ever experienced. At first, he felt frustration while trying to replicate Seo-jun's effortless movements. But slowly, he was infused with the rhythm, like learning to dance in another dimension. Father John had the sensation of flight as he elevated and skittered through the air, tucked and rolled, his body feeling light and pliable, his mind clearing to be filled with joy.

A crowd of students had gathered, and Seo-jun indicated an end to the session. "You are quite skilled," he said to Father John. "You possess the gift. Not everyone does."

"And what is the gift?" Father John asked.

"Not everything needs to be understood." Seo-jun smiled. "Who can explain a flower? Or the internet," he laughed. "How does that work? Sometimes, it is enough to just enjoy what we receive."

"Sensei," Father John began, using the respectful name for a karate master, "can we work out tomorrow?"

"Please, just call me Seo-jun," he replied softly. "I don't use titles here. We are all equal. And yes, it would be an honor to train with you again."

"Wonderful," Father John said. "But no titles? I also noticed you and the rest of the students don't wear belts to designate your rank."

"There was a time when I was very proud to wear the black belt," Seo-jun said, "but then I came to understand that my progress was internal." He tapped two fingers to his chest. "The belt was only about my ego. Something for others to look at, that perhaps made them feel envy or fear. That is not what I teach here. Anyone can buy a black belt, but that does not make them a master. And a master always has more to learn." Father John couldn't help but consider the similarities between a black belt and his cleric's collar, as Seo-Jun motioned at the students. "They are all here for different reasons. Many are looking for self-confidence. Some are mourning. Some want to clear their mind of demons. Others seek community. Some want to feel and guide their bodies in a new way. I want to help them find what they need, not award them a belt to impress others. I've devoted my life to being a guide."

For the next four days, Father John returned every morning to work with Seo-jun, marveling at the transitions he was undergoing. He felt like he had a new body: lighter and faster, free of the physical and mental limitations that had constrained him in the past. Their sparring was more a ballet than anything resembling violence, and he was filled with something new, yet familiar. He recalled his early days in the priesthood, so overflowing with enthusiasm and joy—and what he assumed was the Holy Spirit buoying him—anxious to do God's work. After their final workout, he asked Seo-jun to lunch.

"Tomorrow, I have to return to Santa Pulmo," he said sadly. "But I wanted to thank you. I feel like you somehow saved me."

Seo-jun smiled. "I'm just a guide helping you uncover what you already possessed. I am sure your parish needs you and will be thrilled to have you back," he said. "But you know, you are always welcome in my dojo. Visit anytime, or if you should ever feel the need for a change, come work with me. You have the gift, and you could show others what they don't know they possess. With Covid going away, we will soon be full again. More students are coming in every day, and I will need the help." Father John hugged him and promised to stay in touch.

The next morning, he called Father Leo to let him know what time he would arrive home. "How is it going?" he asked.

"Tough," Father Leo said. "We had a bad incident Sunday. The Men's Group showed up and harassed anyone wearing a mask. Even little kids. Called them sheep, that kind of thing. I'm worried that it will scare people away, and that's the last thing we need. Attendance is already so low. The collection plate was light. And it couldn't be happening at a worse time. The diocese is clamoring for money. They're going to go ahead and settle that suit against Father McDaniel. They should have gotten rid of him when they could, instead of just moving him around. I've heard the number is in the millions. It looks like we will need to close several schools."

Feeling deflated again, Father John dressed in his priest's uniform—black suit and cleric's collar—checked out of the hotel, and was putting his bag in his trunk when a man approached him in the lot. "Hey, Padre," he said with a sneer, "try to keep your hands off the kiddies today."

Father John fought the urge to plant his right foot in the side of the man's face, but instead turned the other cheek and crawled into his car. He sat there for several minutes, breathing hard, reaching inside himself to find any hint of the Holy Spirit that had guided him all these years, but the old emptiness had returned. He craved the sense of lightness and wonder he experienced when training with Seo-jun and considered that the solution might be right in front of him.

He found a parking spot in front of Park Dojo and jumped out of the car, suddenly thrilled at the thought of a new life and calling. The building loomed like a fresh church, and as he had a few days earlier, he stopped outside the window to watch Seo-jun performing his katas, rotating swiftly by himself around the mat. But Seo-jun was not flying or levitating. He was no longer a man possessed with some supernatural ability, just a practiced master moving competently, but without magic. Father John watched in confusion, trying to discern what was happening, when suddenly he realized for the first time that he was seeing the truth.

Overwhelmed, he stumbled back to his car, then ripped off his collar. Seated behind the wheel, he sent Bishop Freemont a text:

Bishop, I am sorry, but I will not be returning to Santa Pulmo or Holy Rosary. The spirit no longer moves me, and the flock deserves better. Please donate my belongings to the parish charity and know that I wish you all the best. John Ellingson.

John drove with no destination in mind, but with fresh clarity, wondering with delight what life would be like without an idol.

Verse XI

DIRTY SANTA

LANCE GLANCED AROUND HIS agent's office, suddenly realizing how shabby the place appeared. Forty years earlier it had been the biggest thrill of his life to sign with Murray Levine. The man that represented Christopher Cross and Captain and Tennille wanted to work with him! However, from the look of the tattered furniture and the dated photos on the wall, it was clear both he and Murray had peaked around 1985.

If he squinted hard, he could see some vestige of young Murray. Of course, the shoulder-length hair, temporarily buoyed by bad implants, had been abandoned in favor of a bald pate two decades earlier. Murray used to flit about town in an ice-white Mercedes 450SL, the vanity plate proclaiming AGENT, clad in his trademark pastel suit with bridge-sized shoulder pads. Now, his vision failing, he tended to Uber. He favored golfing jackets and track pants, with copper-infused support socks and wide shoes that pampered his bunions. After botched cataract surgery, he had given up the battle to don stylish eyewear and peered through huge black framed glasses with comically thick lenses.

Of course, Lance knew that Murray had the same reaction when he looked at him. Lance's heartthrob status had been measured in months, coming to fruition sometime around 1989, when he found himself opening for Men Without Hats at a convention for Terminix franchisees. While he had maintained his hairline, it was now a dusty, mottled gray, a shade commonly seen on a corpse, and his face broadcast the story of a man who had stayed up too late for most of his life. There was a day when he would appear on stage shirtless, young girls frantically reaching up from the front row to trace his rippled abs, their fingers often going lower, but now the only reason to appear undressed would be to pose for the "before" shot in a Weight Watcher's commercial, a gig he would absolutely take if offered.

He had to give Murray credit. The man had stuck with him when any other agent would have dropped him years ago, and Lance didn't blame him for his stalled career. Lance knew he had a common voice and was a mediocre actor, and the fact that he even had one hit and a stint on a sitcom was a fluke. Despite that, Murray had done an admirable job keeping him employed: the eighties reunion tour with Survivor and Rick Springfield; a Time Life infomercial; a reoccurring role as a pedophile music producer on *Law & Order: SVU*; a year in the touring cast of *Rocky Horror Picture Show*. They both sensed the party was ending now. Still, Murray never lost his energy, nor the quintessential agent's talent of spewing bullshit like a Shakespearian soliloquy.

"I've got good news, and great news," Murray blurted out. "Which do you want first?"

It was the game they had been playing for years, Murray overly excited about even the most mediocre offer. Lance couldn't bear to break the tradition. "Might as well start with great," he said.

"You want a little snort first?" Murray motioned at the bottle of Scotch behind his desk, as Lance shook his head no. Years ago, a "little snort" would have meant something completely different, but that was back when both their septa were intact. "Okay, great news. This is for you." He held out a check. "Fourth quarter royalties for 'Dirty Santa,' and as usual, it's a big hit."

Lance looked at the check for $81,000 and smiled. "Dirty Santa" was the gift that just kept giving. He had written the foul Christmas ditty, a song about a distraught woman who has a one-night stand with a man claiming to be Santa, as a joke in 1986 at Murray's urging.

"Do you know how much money Wham makes with that goddamn 'Last Christmas'?" He'd raved years ago. "There's nothing better than a successful holiday song."

Much to their surprise, the tune that took Lance three hours and two bottles of Malbec to create had become a staple in Christmas playlists, not producing Mariah Carey kind of dough but reliably netting at least a hundred grand a year. It had become his retirement plan. As was the tradition with every check, Murray broke into a bad baritone, and Lance joined in:

Dirty Santa, I love you.

Dirty Santa, I know you love me, too.

Dirty Santa, why'd you go and leave me all alone?

"Okay, what's the good news?" Lance said, signaling an end to the duet.

"Offer, offers, offers," Murray said happily, rustling the papers on his desk. "All of a sudden, a lot of people want to be in the Lance Daniels business. Course, having a terrific agent doesn't hurt."

Lance mechanically nodded in agreement. He knew Murray seldom received accolades anymore. He couldn't help but notice one of the "offers" appeared to be a past-due utility bill.

"How about a cruise?" Murray asked. "Beautiful stateroom on a first-class ship. Everything comped. And you only need to do one show a night."

Lance had done a "Hits of the 80s" sailing on Carnival a decade earlier with Cyndi Lauper and Depeche Mode and had come down with the norovirus. He never realized the human body could expel so much liquid from so many orifices. Since then, he'd avoided close quarters, as it exacerbated the hypochondria and germaphobia he'd always suffered.

At least once a week, he woke up with a random pain that he assumed to be the opening volley in a terminal war with his body: a slight cough signaling lung cancer, a headache that must be emanating from a tumor, an intestinal issue suggesting serious inner rot. He'd once mistaken severe athlete's foot for gangrene. Over the years, he'd incorrectly diagnosed himself with AIDS, Ebola, and the even rarer Porphyria (symptoms of which may include purple stool) until he remembered he'd eaten a large beet salad the previous evening. He interpreted any senior moment as a sign of impending dementia. Signing autographs and pressing germy flesh was a part of the job he detested, and though he had been concerned with his waning fame, he didn't miss being crowded and fondled.

"You know I'm not big on boats," he said. "Too many people, and they're filthy."

"Hey," Murray interjected, "this is no shitty Carnival ship. I'm talking the Viva Las Vegas. First class all the way."

"Who's on the venue?" Lance asked.

"Just you. It's your show."

Lance found it hard to believe anyone wanted him to headline, plus he only had about thirty minutes of solid material, and that included stealing two Todd Rundgren songs people might assume were his. "How big is the showroom?"

"Well, it's not the main room. They want you in the lounge. Seats about thirty."

"The lounge," Lance said. "For thirty people? How's the money?"

"Not great, but you get a free cruise," Murray said. "And an open bar."

"And by not great, you mean?"

"Seven hundred for the week. But it's pure profit," Murray said excitedly.

Lance shook his head. "Next. Pass. Can't believe you'd suggest that for a seventy-dollar commission."

"Okay, okay," Murray said, without missing a beat. "This is a good one. Ever been to Santa Pulmo? Beautiful town, right on the coast. They have an incredible little dinner theater. A week rehearsal, and a three-week run in March and early April."

"Sounds better," Lance said. "What's the show?"

"*The Will Rogers Follies*," Murray said, beaming. "A classic."

Lance nodded. A month at the beach sounded nice. "I play Will Rogers?"

"Mmm, no..." Murray said meekly. "You play Clem Rogers, Will's dad. It's better. Not as much to memorize. You can relax and enjoy the beach."

"His dad?" Lance said. "Who plays Will?"

"Scott Baio," Murray said excitedly. "You two will be great. You know Scott. Classy guy. A real pussy hound in the day. You probably ran into him at the Playboy Mansion."

"Scott Baio!" Lance said. "How can I play his father? I can't be more than three or four years older than the guy."

"I'm sure they have a good makeup artist, and you won't need to dye your hair," Murray said, a subtle dig.

"Scott Baio sings?"

"Hey, it's dinner theater in Santa Pulmo," Murray said. "You don't have to be fucking Pavarotti."

"I don't know..."

"Lance, the gig includes your own sweet little house right on the beach, dinner every night in the theater, and twelve grand."

"Twelve grand," Lance repeated. "How do you do, sir?" He bowed and held out a hand. "My name is Clem Rogers."

LANCE WAS CHARMED THE minute he entered Santa Pulmo. The theater owners—a young couple who were frustrated equity actors and appeared in the productions—had recently purchased the establishment, and they gave him the full star treatment.

"I hope you like the house," Leslie said to Lance as she handed him the keys and a map. "It's about ten minutes outside of town. Small but cute, and there's a nice trail to the beach. The people we bought the theater from built it about twenty years ago as a weekend retreat."

Lance thought it sounded perfect for some creative inspiration. He had an idea for a sequel to "Dirty Santa" that had major hit potential. "Trans Santa" seemed perfect for the times. He would be eligible for his SAG pension next year, and if he could add another income stream to the "Dirty Santa" royalties, he could live well. The thought of getting off the road and not having to do any more shitty gigs thrilled him.

An introvert by nature, a career in public had always been painful, especially when he was stopped on the street by people exclaiming, "Hey, aren't you someone famous?" as they searched for a name. Being "almost famous" offered all the hassles of celebrity—loss of privacy, fear of humiliation, security concerns—without any of the perks or money. He looked forward to spending his senior years in semi-seclusion.

Lance was also taken with one of his fellow cast members, Jessie Burdett. The theater booked known actors for one or two roles and filled in the supporting cast with the owners and other locals, and Jessie was a regular performer. On his second day in town, Jessie invited him to the Lazy Owl for coffee, followed by a tour of her bookstore next door.

"I'm impressed," Lance said admiringly. "Actress, singer, business owner, and you're beautiful. Quite a package."

"Thanks, but no need for the LA ass-kissing," Jessie laughed. "I've got a weak voice, move with a middle-aged white woman's rhythm, and barely make a living with the bookstore, but I do have nice skin," she joked. "I love to perform. It's fun to have the theater here."

Lance was charmed and hoped for a little romance while in town. His previous two marriages—both to Hollywood wannabes—had ended in disaster, and he wondered what it would be like to be with a balanced, kind woman not captivated by the concept of fame. He worried about competition when Scott Baio arrived, but Jessie announced, "I hear Chachi is a big Trump guy. Not my style."

Lance professed no political opinions, preferring a "live and let live" philosophy. Much to Murray's consternation, he also detested social media.

"Listen, to be successful now you gotta do the Tweety and Tik Tokky thing," his agent advised. "It's the only way to appeal to the young people."

"Murray, why in the hell would a young person be interested in a washed-up sixty-four-year-old singer that hasn't released an album in thirty years?" he argued.

Murray made an argument involving Bernie Sanders' popularity, but Lance remained unmoved. However, Murray had done well booking this gig. Lance loved the town and settled in comfortably in his new house. The play, while hokey, seemed like it would be up to reasonable tourist town dinner theater standards. Best of all, his relationship with Jessie was progressing. They had dinner a couple times; Lance sent follow-up flowers and was considering his next romantic move.

On the sixth day of rehearsals, the couple that owned the theater brought the cast together for an announcement. "I know everyone has been following the Covid situation," Leslie said. "Unfortunately, due to state mandates, we must cancel the show. Hopefully, this thing will blow over, but there's no way to safely or legally open the theater." She began to weep.

The group was crestfallen but knew there were even bigger financial implications for Leslie and her husband, and nobody wants to chastise a crying woman, so they murmured words of encouragement. Leslie pulled Lance aside as the group broke up.

"Lance, I've got more bad news. Without a show, there is no way we can pay you the second half of your salary." Murray had agreed to a standard half up front, half at the close of the production. "I know we owe you the six thousand, and I would love to pay you, but with no income, we just don't have it right now. Depending on how long this thing lasts, I'm not even sure we're going to make it. We took on a lot of debt when we bought this place."

Lance grimaced. "I understand," he finally said. "Listen, with no performances, do you have plans for the house I'm staying in?"

"No," Leslie said. "We just keep it for visiting cast."

"How about this?" he offered. "Let me stay a couple months in lieu of the six thousand. I'm working on a project, and I really like the place."

Leslie nodded in relief. "Sure, that's a great solution. Stay as long as you like. Maybe this virus will go away quickly, and we can get the show up and running soon. And by the way..." she lowered her voice. "If Scott can't come back, I'd love to have you play Will. He doesn't have much of a singing voice."

Lance smiled and thanked her. He was disappointed but pleased he didn't need to leave Santa Pulmo. A house near the beach was far preferable to his apartment in Burbank.

As he was departing the theater, Scott Baio pulled him aside. "You get stiffed on the second half, too?" he asked.

Lance nodded. "Yep, but what can they do? Can't pay the actors if there's no play."

"That's why I hate doing these little venues," Scott said. "It might suck to work for the studios, but at least you get your money. I've done thirteen pilots that weren't picked up, but I got paid. You have anything lined up?"

Lance shook his head. "How about you?"

"Not yet, but I'm not worried. I'm very popular with the Jesus crowd, and if times get hard, my agent books me at conservative conventions. Sometimes a cruise, and I just need to give a little speech about how I was saved. When times get hard, I tell you, if you're looking to juice your career a bit, you might want to try the Christian conservative angle. Just add a couple Jesus-y songs to the playlist and some 'God Bless America' shit. Wear a MAGA hat onstage. They eat it up," Scott said. "Not much competition. The biggest group to play Trump's inauguration was 3 Doors Down."

"Who?" Lance asked.

"Exactly," Scott laughed. "Hell, if you're willing to play for Trump's events, he'd probably make you ambassador to England. That crowd is hard up for entertainment. Some of the chicks can be hot, especially if you like MILFs. Kinky, too. All kinds of repressed fantasies because quite a few of their husbands are in the closet."

Lance had no desire to make a career shift to play southern mega-churches while cuckolding chubby local Republican couples, but he thanked Scott for the advice before saying goodbye.

Since he wasn't a news guy or social media follower, Lance didn't know much about Covid, and that night he stayed up late reading everything he could find. Given his hypochondria, he'd always assumed mankind was just one short step away from viral disaster—Mother Earth deciding to trim the herd a bit for everyone's benefit—and it occurred to him that this might be the big one.

The next morning, he made two trips to the Costco in Paso Grande, filling his SUV with survivalist's supplies: fifty pounds of rice; twenty pounds of pasta; cases of tomato sauce, tuna, wine, canned vegetables, vodka, beef jerky, rechargeable solar lights, hand sanitizer; gallon jugs of Lysol; a twenty-five-pound canister of Kirkland Signature coffee beans; two hundred rolls of toilet paper; and for some reason, fifteen pair of Champion athletic socks. He had a seventy-five-inch Samsung television, a solar-powered generator, and a freezer delivered, along with eighty pounds of beef, fifteen chickens, and a flat of frozen salmon steaks.

As he was leaving Costco, he noticed the county animal shelter across the street. A large corkboard on the front of the building was plastered with flyers advertising the inmates:

- SPARKY IS GREAT WITH KIDS!
- MR. BOJANGLES IS AN AWESOME FRISBEE PLAYER!
- MISS CLEO LOVES TO CUDDLE AND TAKE NAPS!

There were at least fifty dogs and cats featured—*unwanted posters*—Lance noted sadly. He had not owned a pet since he was ten years old. Though he sometimes dreamt of having a dog, it just didn't make sense, what with his constant time on the road. Given his newfound stable life, he thought it might be time to change that.

He took a tour of the facility and was drawn to a sad little one-eared puppy, a black and white speckled canine of indeterminable breed, cowering in the back of his cage. "What happened to him?" he asked.

"Asshole owner," the woman said. "The guy came after him with a weed wacker."

"Christ," Lance said, holding out a hand. At first, the pup recoiled and trembled in fear, then sniffed a bit, finally allowing himself to be touched. "What's his name?"

"The guy we took him from just called him dog. He wasn't a very nice man." She dropped her voice as if sharing a secret. "So, you could name him." She gave him a hopeful glance.

After completing the adoption paperwork, Lance carried the dog into Petco to stock up, then placed him in the passenger seat of the car. "How do you feel about the name Bingo?" he asked. The pup sniffed and licked his hand, and Lance was officially in love.

The next night, he invited Jessie over for dinner, preparing one of the three Italian dishes he made that would not embarrass him. He introduced her to Bingo, who allowed Jessie to cradle and fawn over him. "Given my singing, I figured a one-eared dog might do better here," Lance quipped. He gave her a tour of all the supplies he had stored in the spare bedroom.

"I suppose next you're going to build an ark," she joked.

When they sat down for dinner, she expressed concern about her bookstore. "I've heard they might force all the businesses to close," she said. "I can't last long financially if that happens. I also worry about my daughter and grandkids. I would hate not to be able to see them."

"It will work out," Lance said soothingly. In the back of his mind, he wondered if things could get serious with Jessie. Since his last divorce, Lance considered dating unfamiliar and often hostile territory. He missed the courtships of his youth, participants wide-eyed and attentive. Now both parties brought electronic cock blockers on the date: pinging phones that interrupted even the most intimate conversations. Lance was annoyed and crestfallen when the woman sitting across from him abruptly stopped the conversation to jump up and photograph the food or waved a hand in his face to apologize after an electronic chirp forced a Pavlovian reaction. "So sorry," she would say, "but I have to take this." Lance assumed it was something urgent, like confirmation of a yoga class or a new Instagram like.

Jessie was different—no phone was visible when they were together—and she looked him in the eye when they talked. She seemed so…sane. He wondered if this was opportunity knocking. "Listen," he said, "they say we need to stay home and create safe little bubbles so the virus doesn't spread. What would you think about us forming a bubble? Just the two of us, or three." He pointed at Bingo. "We can hang out, have meals together. Teach Bingo to fetch. It would save money too, maybe take away some of the financial pressure." He pointed at the keyboard and guitar sitting in the living room. "Could be a musical bubble. Pretend we're Sonny and Cher."

"And which one would you be?" she asked with a straight face before smiling. "Lance, that's sweet," she said. "It sounds wonderful. I would love to sing a duet of 'I've Got You Babe.'" She laughed. "But things are crazy now; I can't really commit to a relationship. I must figure out what is happening with the bookstore. I'm worried about my daughter and her family in Santa Barbara."

"Sure," Lance said, afraid that this might be the last time he saw Jessie for a while.

Luckily, he discovered he was well suited to quarantine. With no houses nearby and no reason to encounter people since everything imaginable could be delivered, he felt reasonably safe as the crisis worsened. A lifetime on the road circulating between lonely hotels had prepared him for isolation. As he traced the progression of the disease, he grew more horrified. He followed the outbreak at the Moonlight Cove retirement home, which quickly spread through the little town. He was baffled by the public response to the emergency. He could not imagine why people would treat the pandemic as if it were a hoax and politicize simple things like wearing a mask. As he watched YouTube videos of irate anti-maskers arguing and assaulting store clerks, he grew more despondent over the future of humanity. "A lot of people are just too dumb to live," he commented to Bingo, realizing he now conversed with his dog on a regular basis. Bingo's ear perked up, hoping they were discussing a walk or food.

As the weeks passed, he began to see a bright side of Covid and used the opportunity to try all the things his life had never allowed. He subscribed to every streaming service and began to catch up on all the television he had missed over the years: *The Sopranos, The Wire, Game of Thrones, Curb Your Enthusiasm*; documentaries on all the wars and a dozen presidents; and the movies cinephiles regarded as the best in history.

Bingo would sit next to him on the couch, sharing popcorn and sometimes barking at the screen when another dog appeared. He took cooking classes with Gordon Ramsey, brushed up on his guitar skills with Joe Satriani, listened to Steve Martin lecture on comedy, and took singing lessons from Christina Aguilera. He had never been a big reader, but now he committed to completing at least one book a week.

In June, he received a call from Leslie informing him that the theater was officially broke, and they were putting it up for sale. He offered to buy the house, and after a pleasant negotiation, they agreed on a price. Unlike most entertainers, Lance had always been more interested in earning than spending, and he had a reasonable nest egg for the down payment. With the low interest rates, he figured he could swing it. He'd made the decision this was the place he wanted to spend the rest of his life.

He planted a garden, consulting online forums to determine the ideal crops. Now, the first hour of his day was spent weeding, clipping, and battling the predators that attacked his lettuce and tomatoes.

One day he had a call from Murray. "I've got incredible news. Just incredible." Lance's one hit from 1985, "Margarita Kisses," a pulpy love song about a man who meets his soulmate on a Mexican beach, had been licensed by a tequila company for their advertising. "A hundred grand a year, two-year contract, with an option to extend," Murray shouted. "Who's the best damn agent in the world?"

"You are," Lance replied, stunned by the new financial windfall. He used part of the proceeds to place solar panels and a battery system on the house, now obsessed with moving off the grid as much as possible.

By mid-July, he realized that, except for his daily walks on the beach, he had not left the property in months. His only outside contact was to wave at Al, the UPS man, and a weekly Zoom with Murray. He began to wonder about his mental health. Bingo was the only living being he conversed with, and he doubted the dog was a good judge of his sanity. He thought it might be time to venture outside the house.

He'd read that Jessie and her band were doing performances on the lawn in front of Moonlight Cove, and even though it had been a Covid hotspot, he figured he could stay in his car and watch safely from a distance. He wondered if Jessie might be willing to reconsider his proposal.

The night before the concert, he glanced at his reflection. For the last decade, he'd winced whenever he viewed himself. He wished he could go back in time and convince young Lance to cherish his brown locks, smooth complexion, flat stomach, illimitable energy, and effortless, firm erections. He savored favorite erotic memories, knowing a body beset with sagging skin, an artificial knee, aging's strange odors, and his recent inability to stay awake past midnight could never replicate them. He would encourage his twenty-five-year-old self to view his precious twenties and thirties the way a child perceives a roller coaster, a thrilling ride that is always too short. Unfortunately, the only way to understand life's unfair velocity was to experience the breakneck speed that humans move through their prime years.

He realized a little grooming might be in order. He shaved and found an online video on how to cut your own hair. He soon discovered there was a reason that even hair stylists didn't give themselves haircuts. He now resembled the Jeff Daniels character in *Dumb and Dumber* and pulled his hat down to cover the hatchet job.

The lot at Moonlight Cove was filling up when he arrived, which made him queasy. He couldn't help trying to calculate the odds that the occupants of the car next to his might be infected. When Jessie and her band began to play, he masked up, opened his sunroof, and popped his head out the top so he could hear. Jessie saw him, smiled, and waved. However, the people in the car beside him got out of their vehicle unmasked and leaned on their hood. As they sang along to "Hit Me With Your Best Shot," Lance was positive he could see spittle flying from their lips. He envisioned diseased pustules launched into the breeze to waft across the crowd like lethal gas. Now they were dancing beside the car, and Lance realized he was in a radioactive fallout zone. If one of them turned slightly, which seemed highly likely as they shimmied hard to "Love is a Battlefield," he would be directly in the path of salivic napalm.

He dropped back into his vehicle and shut the sunroof. Since he couldn't hear the music, he figured the concert was a risky bust and opted to leave. As he was backing up, Jessie gave him a confused look. It occurred to him that they couldn't have had a real conversation anyway. As much as he missed her, with all her public appearances, she was now a health threat. He felt relieved to be safe when he arrived back at the beach house. Bingo, unaccustomed to any separation, whined with joy and jumped into his arms when he walked in the door.

For the next ten days, Lance took his temperature at four-hour intervals, positive he would discover a raging fever from contracting Covid at the concert. He'd been experiencing the strange sleep patterns many people suffered since Corona began, waking up several times during the night, but now found himself staring at the ceiling at four a.m., trying to figure out if the slight pain in his chest was real—the onset of the virus—or just a result of laying wrong. After two weeks without any outside contact, he began to calm down. "I think I dodged a bullet," he told Bingo, "but to be safe, it has got to be just you and me until this thing blows over."

As the months passed, Lance realized there was much he enjoyed about the pandemic. No outside contact meant no exposure to any kind of virus, and he luxuriated waking up every day without any hint of a cold or the flu. He was thrilled to flex his mind and body in new ways. He learned to speak Spanish from an app and took online art history courses. Since fitness seemed to play an important role in surviving the disease, he had committed to getting into great shape. He bought a Peloton bike and rode religiously for an hour each day, not only enjoying the workout but also the interaction with the instructors. He walked Bingo on the beach, finishing the jaunt with twenty pushups and fifty crunches. He realized what an unhealthy diet he'd eaten while on the road, and now his garden, supplemented with a little protein he ordered from a grass-fed ranch, provided most of his sustenance. By November, he'd dropped twenty pounds and had to trade in his oversized wardrobe for a far preferable collection of slim-cut jogging pants and sweatshirts.

November signaled the beginning of the Christmas music season, and Lance was excited about the release of "Trans Santa." None of the major labels had been interested in the song, but given the success of "Dirty Santa," a respectable producer had worked with Lance to release it. The following week, Murray called.

"Jesus, kid, all hell is breaking loose over your song," he said. "Apparently, a lot of folks in the LBDO community are offended," he said.

"You mean LGBTQ?" Lance said.

"Yeah, whatever," Murray said. "The gays. That whole group. They don't like the song, and they've organized a boycott. Says it is offensive. Course, I don't agree, I thought it was some of your best work, but you know how things are now. Spotify, Apple, and Pandora took it down."

"Jesus," Lance said. "I didn't mean to offend anyone. It was supposed to be funny." Suddenly he realized what a silly mistake he'd made, like a sweet grandpa that inadvertently makes a racist comment. "I have LGBTQ friends. I would never make fun of them."

"Of course you wouldn't," Murray consoled him. "It's different now. These kids on the web go after people like a pack of wild dogs. Have you Googled yourself lately?"

Lance went to his computer, shocked to see the vitriol aimed against him. "What the hell?" He shouted into the phone. "People are calling me homophobic and a Nazi. Some woman says I exposed myself to her at the Olive Garden in Billings, MT. Murray, I promise you I have never been in an Olive Garden or Billings, MT. None of this is true."

"I know, I know," Murray said. "It's a new world. The internet's an outlet for the mean and crazy."

"Well, fine then," Lance said. "Bury the damn song. I'm sorry I ever wrote it."

"It gets worse," Murray said. "They've also pulled 'Dirty Santa.' They're saying it's anti-women."

"What?" Lance said in amazement. "I love women. That song has been around for thirty-five-years. Why is it a problem now?"

"Some people think the Santa character is a predator. Like I said, new world. That leads me to 'Margarita Kisses.' The tequila company is taking a lot of flak for being associated with you, and they've pulled it. They will pay out the contract, but it won't be renewed."

"Jesus, Murray, this isn't fair. One mistake shouldn't sink my career. I'll apologize."

"Sorry, kid. Right now, nobody wants to be in the Lance Daniels business. The whole cancel culture thing. Give it some time. This will blow over, and people will forget about it. Those songs are too good to be put away forever."

For the next hour, Lance read the hate directed against him online. The accusations were stunning and cruel. A stylist he was sure he had never met claimed he used racist language while filming a music video in 1986. A woman he might have dated once twenty years earlier said he made disparaging remarks about a gay waiter. Ex-wife number two, who now worked as a dog groomer in Medford, Oregon, and appeared to have a substance abuse problem, did an interview with the *Huffington Post*, claiming he was a misogynist, most likely because he had been abused by his mother.

"This is all nonsense," Lance yelled. A clickbait site with a photo altered to make Lance look sinister, featured the headline "MEET HOLLYWOOD'S MOST HATED STARS." "At least they called me a star," he muttered to Bingo, who yelped in hope a treat was forthcoming. Hulu, which still ran his old sitcom, announced they were pulling it off the air. Baffled, he shut his computer and pledged never to Google himself again. "The whole world has gone nuts," he said. "Good riddance."

A few days before Christmas, Lance was shocked when he logged onto his regular Zoom with Murray. His friend looked weak and sickly. "What's going on?" he asked.

"Jesus, kid, I caught the Rona. Played golf last week with Johnny Earhart, and it turns out he caught it from his son who was home from college. We were idiots. Wore masks around everyone else but figured the two of us were safe. I think he even took a sip from my beer. He called me the day after we played to give me the good news, and I was sick within a couple days. Serves me right for hanging around with that degenerate. What kind of eighty-year-old has a kid in college?"

"Oh no," Lance said. "You're not looking good. What does the doctor say?"

"I'll be fine," Murray said, "but don't catch it. It's a bitch."

Three days later, Murray's wife called to inform him Murray had passed away the previous night from a stroke brought on by Covid. Even though his health had been dicey for a long time, Lance was stunned and heartbroken. The man he'd spoken to every week for almost forty years was gone, and so it seemed, was the biggest chapter in his life.

That night Lance dug through the storeroom to find "the memory box," with framed pictures, plaques, and other memorabilia he never found the time to unpack. Looking at the photos, he realized most of them included Murray. There was a shot at the 1985 Grammys, Lance and Murray flanked by Sheena Easton and Stevie Wonder. Lance and Murray smoking cigars by the pool at the Four Seasons, Christmas 1986, celebrating the success of "Dirty Santa." Toasting Murray at his surprise fiftieth birthday party at the Hotel Bel-Air, arms encircling both of their first wives. Lance didn't have an important memory from the last forty years that didn't involve his friend.

Murray's wife opted not to have a service, and instead, people gathered online to pay their last respects. Lance was happy Murray could not see how it all ended.

Lance remembered standing next to him a few years earlier at David Cassidy's service. "Good turnout," Murray commented, motioning at the crowd. "You know, this is the mark of a good run in our business—how many people come to pay their respects. You should have seen George Burn's funeral. Biggest crowd he ever had. You have a long career, and the people you touched come to say goodbye. Wish I could see my own send-off. Hopefully, there will be a packed house with people I've helped make successful." Lance wouldn't want Murray to know there were only about a dozen friends saying farewell.

A month later, Lance read a short obituary in the *Santa Pulmo Explorer* announcing Jessie Burdett had died in Santa Barbara. He was shocked. He'd fantasized about getting back together with her when all this ended. The paper featured several photos of Jessie: a recent shot taken while she and her band played in front of Moonlight Cove, a picture taken in her bookshop, and the most shocking to Lance, a promotional photo of the entire cast taken before they canceled *The Will Rogers Follies*. Lance was standing close to her, wearing a ridiculous wide-brimmed hat, one hand around her waist. He remembered the day, leaning in so her hair tickled his chin, and he could smell the hint of lavender he always associated with Jessie.

Despondent, he took Bingo for a long walk on the beach. "I guess that's it," he said to the dog. "Just you and me. How does a guy get to be my age and only have two friends?" he asked sadly. Bingo sniffed at a rotting clump of seaweed, sneezed, and buried his face in the cuff of Lance's pants.

"Hughes residence, two packages," a soft voice announced as the UPS truck turned into the driveway. Al initially had trouble adapting to the self-driving vehicles, but once he gained trust, he had to admit it was a nice way to travel. The electric truck was silent and rode comfortably on an adjustable air suspension. Package data was downloaded as it was loaded, the computer charted the most efficient driving route, and Al could sit back in the oversized seat and enjoy the scenery.

UPS drones now dispatched most packages, with heavier and more specialized deliveries left to a human touch. Al had been surprised he had made it all the way to retirement age, as about half the workforce had been eliminated over the years. However, with his sixty-seventh birthday looming, he had made it and was looking forward to a generous pension and a lot of golf.

Al and Chris, the recruit he was training to take over the route, jumped out of the truck. A sensor connected to fobs on their brown uniforms unlocked and raised the rear door. A conveyor system scanned the two packages and moved them within easy reach.

"I hope you appreciate how good you have it," Al joked. "I used to have to climb all over the dirty old trucks to move heavy boxes. Threw my back out every few weeks."

Chris carried the packages toward the delivery hub, a metal container installed on the front porch to accommodate both human and drone deliveries. The hub recognized his fob and unlocked the door. A camera recorded him as he placed the box inside and sent a delivery notification to the residents after re-locking the cabinet. They climbed back in the truck and veered onto a dirt road heading toward the beach, the voice announcing, "Daniels' residence, four packages."

"Mr. Daniels gets a lot of deliveries," Al said. "He never leaves the property, so he depends on us."

"He never goes anywhere?" Chris asked.

"He freaked out during Covid and must have decided he liked quarantining, because in all these years, I don't think he's ever left the place. I see him sometimes, and he waves, but he prefers if you keep your distance. He's a good guy. Sometimes, he leaves me a basket of produce from his garden. He grows great tomatoes and figs. Leaves a bottle of champagne on Christmas. Just don't ever get closer than ten feet. It makes him uncomfortable."

"Sounds nuts," Chris said. "He hasn't left his house in six years?"

Al laughed. "I'm not talking about Covid-35. He's been cooped up since Covid-19."

"Nineteen?" Chris said. "Are you kidding? I was a little kid. I barely remember it. That was like twenty years ago."

"Twenty-two, to be exact."

"He lives by himself?" Chris asked.

"Yep. He's had a few dogs, but from what I can tell, he's a loner. He used to be kind of a big deal. You're too young to remember, but he was a star. He sang and was on a TV show. The girls loved him."

"How old is he?" Chris asked.

"Got to be in his mid-eighties, but he looks good."

"And he lives like a hermit?"

"Yep. Covid-19 changed people. Changed everything," Al said.

LANCE WAS WORKING IN the garden when his phone pinged, announcing packages had been locked in the delivery hub. He was expecting something important but couldn't remember what. For the last year, his memory seemed to come and go with the tide. *Maybe pills from the Amazon pharmacy? Dog food?* As he rounded the corner of the house, cane in hand, a little brown terrier at his heel, the UPS truck was pulling out of the driveway. Al waved, as did another man he didn't recognize, and Lance returned the gesture. *Maybe he did know the man,* Lance thought as the truck disappeared behind a dust cloud. He remembered talking to Al through the screen door a week or so earlier, Al informing him that he was retiring and there would be someone new on the route. He might have met him then. It was getting more difficult to tell fact from fiction, recollections from dreams.

But that's okay, Lance figured. His mind usually wandered to wonderful places. Whether they were memories or fantasies didn't matter at his age, as long as they felt good, like watching a favorite movie. Except sometimes Lance had the feeling he had starred in the film.

He'd see himself on a stage, young and beautiful, thousands of people cheering and holding up lighters in the dark, as if he were floating through stars. Sometimes, he recalled reclining on a beach, sipping margaritas with a beautiful woman as a sweet song played. His favorites were the holiday visions: Christmas dinner with his folks in the tiny dining room they only used on special occasions, then sprinting toward the presents under the tree. And the one that haunted and thrilled him: He was at a Christmas party, somewhere warm because they were sitting outside by a pool. He and the other man, clad in funny Santa hats, were laughing, drinking, and smoking thick cigars. They were both young and handsome, and people—even famous people—would stop to say hello and shake their hands as if they were important. He couldn't remember the man's name, but he sensed they were friends—*no, more than that, best friends*—and they were celebrating. Not just Christmas, something else, something important and wonderful. They broke into song, the man's voice deep and warm, and somehow pleasantly off-key:

Dirty Santa, I love you.
Dirty Santa, I know you love me, too.
Dirty Santa, why'd you go and leave me all alone?

www.ingramcontent.com/pod-product-compliance
Lightning Source LLC
Chambersburg PA
CBHW030743120726
47947CB00013B/8

* 9 7 8 1 6 4 4 2 8 5 0 7 7 *